Penguin Books

The SHINY GUYS

DOUG MACLEOD left his full-time TV production job in 2002 to focus on writing books for children and young adults. So far he's written seven novels for Penguin. His last novel, *The Life of a Teenage Body-Snatcher*, was an Honour Book in the Australian Children's Book Council Awards, 2011. He lives and works in St Kilda, in Melbourne. In 2008 The Australian Writers' Guild presented him with the Fred Parsons Award for Contribution to Australian Comedy. Despite this, *The Shiny Guys* is a serious book without too many jokes.

Shortlisted: 2012 Victorian Premier's Literary Awards
– Prize for Writing for Young Adults

OTHER BOOKS BY DOUG MACLEOD

The Life of a Teenage Body-Snatcher

Siggy and Amber

The Clockwork Forest

Kevin the Troll

Leon Stumble's Book of Stupid Fairytales
(illustrated by Craig Smith)

I'm Being Stalked by a Moonshadow

Tumble Turn

Spiky Spiky My Pet Monkey
(illustrated by Craig Smith)

On the Cards
(illustrated by Craig Smith)

Sister Madge's Book of Nuns
(illustrated by Craig Smith)

The Birdsville Monster
(illustrated by Craig Smith)

The
SHINY
GUYS

DOUG MacLEOD

PENGUIN BOOKS

Published by the Penguin Group
Penguin Group (Australia)
707 Collins Street, Melbourne, Victoria 3008, Australia
(a division of Pearson Australia Group Pty Ltd)
Penguin Group (USA) Inc.
375 Hudson Street, New York, New York 10014, USA
Penguin Group (Canada)
90 Eglinton Avenue East, Suite 700, Toronto, Canada ON M4P 2Y3
(a division of Pearson Penguin Canada Inc.)
Penguin Books Ltd
80 Strand, London WC2R 0RL England
Penguin Ireland
25 St Stephen's Green, Dublin 2, Ireland
(a division of Penguin Books Ltd)
Penguin Books India Pvt Ltd
11 Community Centre, Panchsheel Park, New Delhi – 110 017, India
Penguin Group (NZ)
67 Apollo Drive, Rosedale, Auckland 0632, New Zealand
(a division of Pearson New Zealand Ltd)
Penguin Books (South Africa) (Pty) Ltd
Rosebank Office Park, Block D, 181 Jan Smuts Avenue, Parktown North,
Johannesburg, 2196, South Africa
Penguin (Beijing) Ltd
7F, Tower B, Jiaming Center, 27 East Third Ring Road North,
Chaoyang District, Beijing 100020, China

Penguin Books Ltd, Registered Offices: 80 Strand, London, WC2R 0RL, England

First published by Penguin Group (Australia), 2012

3 5 7 9 10 8 6 4 2

Text copyright © Estuary Productions, 2012.

The moral right of the author has been asserted.

Cover and text design by Karen Scott © Penguin Group (Australia)
Cover images by Veer and Shutterstock

Typeset in 10/15pt Trump Mediaeval by Post Pre-Press Group, Brisbane, Queensland
Colour separation by Splitting Image Colour Studio, Clayton, Victoria
Printed and bound in Australia by McPherson's Printing Group, Maryborough, Victoria

National Library of Australia
Cataloguing-in-Publication data:

MacLeod, Doug, 1959–
Shiny guys / Doug MacLeod.
9780143565307 (pbk.)
For young adults.
A823.3

penguin.com.au

This story is set in 1985.
Psychiatric wards are different today.

CHAPTER I

I share a room with a man who snores. Every night I hear the snorts and rattles, as annoying as a mosquito in my ear. The man is called Len and he dislikes me. When he snores, I go to his bed, reach under the cover and pull his big toe. This usually stops the racket. If I'm lucky, Len doesn't wake up. Usually I'm unlucky. He wakes and curses me. He's spoken to the doctors about it. He wants me to sleep somewhere else. I do too. But there is a shortage of beds in Ward 44. As soon as a bed becomes available, a new person moves in. There's no playing musical beds and moving patients from one room to another in Ward 44. The nurses don't have time for that.

Len is weaving a basket. It's his favourite thing in the world. He keeps it close to his bed as if he's afraid someone is going to steal it. Some of the patients are so odd, that could actually happen.

I couldn't believe it when I found out about the basket-weaving. It's 1985. We've launched the space shuttle, we have amazing fax machines, but we still weave baskets in Ward 44. I thought that went out with leeches.

We also have electro-convulsive therapy, or shock treatment, which terrifies me. I haven't had that, and nor will I. My parents have to consent for that to happen. They assured me they haven't and never will.

I'm sitting at a laminated table with the other inmates, eating breakfast. A new girl walks into the dining room and sits on her own. She looks about sixteen. The creases in the legs and arms of her grey issue pyjamas are sharp and military. We're all given two pairs of grey pyjamas without pockets when we arrive. The girl has the spare pair in her lap. I don't take my pyjamas to the laundry as often as I should. I rarely have nice sharp creases. That's a black mark against me.

The inmates of Ward 44 come in all shapes and sizes. Some are old, some are young, but we are united in one respect. Our brains don't work. Or rather, they *do* work, just not in a way society finds acceptable. We have mental problems, some more serious than others.

Government contractors built Ward 44. That's why it looks like a school, with grey linoleum in the corridors, light green walls and white window frames. There are fifteen bedrooms, each with two single beds. Bedrooms don't have doors. Anyone walking along the corridor can look in. There's a small basement with a laundry at the northern end of the ward.

The dining room is as big as four bedrooms. It has red laminate tables and thirty-six chairs, even though there are only thirty patients. The six extra chairs bother me. Why are they here? The other wards in the hospital could use them, but here we are hogging them in Ward 44. We even have a courtyard with benches and a few plants. We're spoiled. I should be grateful, but I'm not.

The dining room smells of toast, coffee and disinfectant. The cutlery is plastic and harmless. There is an urn for coffee and another for tea. Len has tea. He looks at me darkly as he pours himself a lukewarm cup. I woke Len up last night when I pulled his big toe.

'Little prick,' he mutters.

Len sits with Val, who keeps telling people she is an alcoholic, as if any of us care. Len possibly likes Val because she flatters. Someone must have told her it's a good way to make friends. The very first thing she said to me was that I had sparkling eyes and hair. My eyes don't sparkle and neither does my hair. Right now she's probably telling Len how musical his voice sounded when he said 'little prick'. Val is deeply religious. She asked me once if I had found Our Lord Jesus Christ. I told her no. He must be in a different ward.

I'm curious about the girl. She flinches and turns her head a little, as if trying to see something out of the corner of her eye. I think she may be here for the same reason I am.

Mango puts his tray down next to mine. He has a solid build and dirty blond hair. His pyjamas are less well maintained than mine. He's carrying a tray with orange juice and a mountain of breakfast cereal.

'Hello, mental case,' I say.

'Hello, spazzo,' Mango replies.

Mango is here because he has an attachment disorder. He grabs people from behind and holds on. He can't help it. If patients are bothered they know to call a nurse. I don't. The regular activities in Ward 44 are not thrilling and I'm never in a hurry to go anywhere.

Mango eats quickly. He takes big spoonfuls of cereal and milk runs down his chin. I'm not sure if this is a condition or not. When you're in a psychiatric ward (I've been in Ward 44 for four weeks) it's difficult to have a sense of perspective.

Shamita, the Indian nurse, places a paper cup in front of each patient. Mango's cup contains three tablets – two red and one yellow. My cup contains a yellow tablet and a blue tablet. I take the yellow tablet three times a day and the blue tablet twice. At night I take five capsules. I hated the yellow tablets at first. They made me too drowsy to read, and that's what I enjoy doing most. I'm used to them now, and reading as well as ever, mainly science fiction.

I look across at the new girl. She's probably freaked out because she thinks she's insane. That's the first thing you worry about when you arrive here. You believe that you're genuinely insane, but you just didn't realise it. You might have been eccentric or just a tiny bit weird – but never *insane*. The chances are, you're not. Before long, you realise this. By then the yellow tablets kick in.

I'm not insane, but I still see things out of the corner of my eye: red shining shapes as big as a man. I see them when I'm awake and when I'm asleep. I call them the shiny guys.

Mango puts down his spoon.

'I had the dream again,' he says, 'about being locked in the impossible cupboard.'

'I'm sorry about that.'

'The doctor says I need to try something. Before I go to sleep, I'm supposed to think about the dream and give it a happy ending. I have to make up an ending that's not horrible. That way the dream will change and I won't be freaked. But I can't think of any way to give that dream a happy ending. Can you?'

Mango is asking me because he thinks I'm clever.

'What if you won the lotto?' I suggest.

'What good is that if I'm stuck in a cupboard?'

'What if there's a naked lady in there with you?'

Mango thinks about this because he likes naked ladies.

'It's a small cupboard. Not very deep. It would be a complete waste of a naked lady.'

'What if you turn into a cockroach? Then you'd be able to crawl out of the cupboard.'

'Yeah, but I'd be a cockroach. That's not a happy ending.'

'It is if you meet a lady cockroach waiting outside and you have sex.'

Mango smiles even though he's bothered by the memory of the dream. He likes it when I use expressions like 'have sex' rather than the more obvious words. Sometimes he even copies the way I talk.

'I don't want to *have sex* with a cockroach,' says Mango.

'You would if you were a cockroach.'

'None of those endings are any good,' he says. 'But thanks anyway.'

My gigantic friend makes a sad noise and runs his calloused hand through his hair. It sticks up but still looks good.

'I want it to stop,' he says. 'You don't know what it's like to have this bad dream night after night.'

But I do know. I dream of the shining red guys on the edge of my vision. In my dreams they're indistinct and formless, but I know what they're thinking. Their thoughts turn into words. They are not nice.

The new girl stares at the breakfast tray in front of her as if she doesn't know what to do with a slice of toast, a bowl of breakfast cereal and a cup of orange juice. It was the same for me when I arrived.

Shamita places the paper cup in front of the girl and won't leave until the girl has downed her drugs. The girl does this awkwardly and Shamita goes away. Then the girl flinches and looks over her shoulder, just like I do. We have something in common, I'm sure of it. I have to speak with her.

I leave Mango and casually sit in a chair next to the new girl.

'I can get you jam,' I say.

The girl looks at me in confusion. She's got one of those baby-faces, with wide-apart eyes and a small nose. She's very thin. Her hair is lank and dark. She hasn't been taking good care of it. If I look hard I could probably see dandruff, so I don't look hard. Some people would find her pretty, even with the bad hair.

'Would you like some jam for your toast?' I say. 'I have my personal supply of bubble packs. I'm Colin. What's your name?'

'Anthea,' she whispers.

The most important thing is that she doesn't get electro-convulsive therapy. I've escaped it because the doctors can't zap me unless Mum and Dad sign a special form. They haven't. No one is frying my brain. Anthea looks the same age as me, so the doctors will have to get her parents' permission as well.

'Ring your parents,' I say. 'Tell them you don't want ECT.'

'What?'

'Tell your parents you don't want electro-convulsive therapy. You have parents? Or guardians? Or –'

'Of course I have parents.'

'Well, not everyone does. Mango doesn't. And don't worry; you're not a freak. I see those things too. Out of the corner of my eye.'

She draws away from me. 'What are you talking about?'

'I've seen the way you move your eyes and your head. We've got the same thing. Shiny guys, right? Would you like jam?'

'Go away,' she says loudly.

'Okay,' I say. 'No jam.'

I've made a spectacle in the dining room. Some patients

chewing toast without jam (because I've stolen it) look at me and shake their heads. Somehow I've managed to upset the new arrival. Two nurses come, Tim and Keith. They ask Anthea if she is all right. She freezes them out.

Anthea is staring at her breakfast again, as if trying to eat it telepathically. I resume my place alongside Mango.

'What did you tell her?' Mango asks, wiping milk from his chin. 'Did you mention the ECT?'

'Yes.'

'Good. She's beautiful and I don't want anyone to zap her brain. What's her name?'

'Anthea.'

'I might go over and say hello.'

'That's probably not a good idea. Not yet.'

'I'll just say hello.'

'Mango, you and I know what could happen. You *might* just say hello. But you might also put your arms around her and not let go. It's her first day. She'll be scared to death.'

'You mentioned the shiny guys, didn't you?'

'Maybe a bit.'

'Man, even *I* was freaked out by the shiny guys when you told me.'

'Yeah. It was probably a mistake to bring them up.'

'Are you going to finish that?' He points at my breakfast cereal.

'No, you have it.'

I pass my half-empty bowl to Mango. When he's done eating, he burps and looks around.

'I don't see Grace anywhere,' he says.

'I think she was discharged.'

'But she was totally spastic.'

You could tell Grace was on non-prescription drugs. She kept laughing at things that weren't funny. It was a mean laugh. She had visitors who sat with her in the courtyard. They looked sickly and pallid, with cheap tattoos, just like Grace. Some of the patients were jealous that so many people visited Grace. I told them that the visitors were probably drug mules. That made the patients feel better.

My file lies open on the desk.

'So, Colin. Is there anything you'd like to tell me?' Dr Parkinson asks. He has grey curly hair and a face that is like a child's, all pink and shiny.

'Not really.'

'How do you feel?'

I shrug. 'Okay.'

'You haven't been eating. You still find it hard to leave your bed and face the day.'

'So does everyone here.'

'Only the depressed ones. Have you called your parents since we last spoke?'

'No.'

'You really should call them, Colin.'

I look at the pen caddy on Dr Parkinson's desk. A big black texta rests amongst the pens and pencils. I want that texta. It won't be long before I get it.

'What happened to Grace?' I ask.

'She was sent to a *traditional* hospital that can perhaps do more for her than we can.'

Ward 44 is *not* traditional. It's Dr Parkinson's pride and joy. He says the patients are on a unique journey. We don't just rely on doctors and nurses. We also help *one another* to get well. That's the theory, anyway. He's written articles about it and given lectures. He says we're all in it together, though I notice he doesn't walk around in grey pyjamas.

'Colin, what did you say to the new arrival today?'

'I was just saying hello. Being helpful.'

'Did you tell her anything that might have upset her?'

'I just told her that you aren't allowed to give her ECT unless her parents agree.'

Dr Parkinson sighs. He's been doing a lot of that lately.

'I wish you'd trust us. Of course we will consult with Anthea's parents if we consider that electro-convulsive therapy might be beneficial. If they object, we will find an alternative means of treatment.'

'You mean drugs, like the ones I'm on?'

'People here are on many different forms of medication. And some patients are undergoing ECT with very positive results.'

'Which ones?'

'I can't tell you that.'

'I bet I can guess.'

'I doubt it. ECT isn't the demon people presume it is. That film with Jack Nicholson didn't help.'

'*One Flew Over the Cuckoo's Nest.*'

'You've seen it?'

I nod.

'It's very misleading. It was irresponsible to make such a film.'

I keep eying the texta. It looks new. I imagine holding it in my hand, taking off the cap, enjoying the chemical smell.

'How are the shiny guys?' asks Dr Parkinson. 'Do you still see them?'

I nod.

Dr Parkinson tilts back in his chair. It would be very funny if the chair tipped and he went arse over tit. I like it when things like that happen. I almost smile at the thought.

'I think you still blame yourself,' Dr Parkinson says. 'If you stopped blaming yourself for what happened, I wouldn't be at all surprised if the hallucinations also stopped.'

He tilts forward and rests his arms on the desk. There will be no slapstick today.

'I don't think I should take so many pills. They're not working.'

'Then we might have to try something else.'

'Can't I just stop taking the pills?'

'We can look at reducing the dose. You can't stop taking your medication altogether. There are withdrawal symptoms. As for the bad dreams, I do have a technique that might help.'

'Is that where I imagine a happy ending?'

Dr Parkinson nods. 'You have a good imagination. I'm sure you'll think of one.'

My daily session over, I leave Dr Parkinson and his brand-new texta. Maybe he's right? Maybe the shiny guys will go away if I stop blaming myself? But I'm the one who wrecked our family. My parents will never stop blaming me, so why should I?

CHAPTER 2

In the Flinders Ranges there is a place called Pichi Richi
Pass. Mum and Dad decided they wanted to go camping
there. They weren't outdoorsy people. Bugs frightened
my mother. They frightened me too, although I liked
grasshoppers because of their friendly faces. But my parents were determined that we should become a family
that camps, so they bought a second-hand trailer tent.

It was a long drive to the Flinders Ranges. Dad kept
pointing out fascinating landforms that really weren't
that fascinating. I practised the magic tricks I'd been
teaching myself. I was getting good. My sister Briony
couldn't work out how I could take a perfectly normal
deck of cards, fan them out, get her to choose one, replace
it in the deck, shuffle, then find her card every time. She
kept falling for my most basic tricks, like palming a coin
so that it magically disappears. She loved it when I pro-
duced the coin from various unusual places, usually out
of her ear or nose, but sometimes I'd get her to lift her

backside off the seat so I could pull the coin out of there. We laughed like crazy and Mum told me that she would never have bought me the magic book if she'd known I would use it to make coins appear out of my sister's bottom. She told us to read quietly instead.

I took out my copy of *Pebble in the Sky*, a science fiction novel by Isaac Asimov. Briony read one of Mum's magazines. She asked Mum for a pen so that she could do the crossword. Mum handed a pen to Briony. But Briony left the crossword alone. In the magazine, there was an advertisement for a health spa, showing a lady in a white dressing gown, with cucumber slices over her eyes. She was smiling in ecstasy, as if having salad on your face was the most wonderful feeling in the world. The caption underneath the picture was, *Spoil yourself this winter*. Briony drew over one of the letters and showed me her handiwork. She had crossed the letter P out of the caption. Now it read, *Soil yourself this winter*. In my mind was an image of the elegant cucumber lady crapping herself. I tried hard not to laugh, because I didn't want to startle Dad and make him run off the road. But Briony had invented such a good joke, it was impossible to hold back.

I guffawed.

Mum issued an ultimatum. We were not to make a *single* noise until we reached the Flinders Ranges. Dad had a better idea. He suggested that Mum put the *Goon Show* tape in the cassette player. It was our favourite tape, full of stupid songs we knew off by heart. After a minute or two, even Mum was singing to 'The Ying Tong Song'.

We reached the caravan park at Pichi Richi Pass. Night fell as we set up the trailer tent. We weren't the only people who wanted to get away from the big smoke. There were dozens of other tents and caravans. For dinner we ate roast chicken rolls and cake under the stars. Dad told us that the light from the stars had taken millions of years to reach us. For all we knew, some of the stars we were looking at might have burned out long ago. I thought of *Pebble in the Sky*, set fifty thousand years in the future, when the earth is a miserable radioactive planet, and wondered what the night sky would look like then.

The next morning we got up early, just after sunrise. A light rain fell. Dad said it was spitting and Briony thought that was funny – that the sky would want to spit at us. After breakfast, we prepared to go bushwalking. It was cloudy, but Mum made us cover every part of our exposed bodies in sunscreen. Our four backpacks contained bottles of water, trail mix, chocolate bars, insect repellent and extra sunscreen. We wore green cloth caps to protect us from falling spiders and tucked our tracksuit pants into our socks so that leeches wouldn't get us. We tried our hardest to look like professional bushwalkers, but we probably looked like professional idiots. In the car was a big white first-aid box with a red cross on the side. Mum wondered if we should take some antiseptic cream or bandages, but Dad told her not to bother. We weren't going far.

Dad had a pamphlet of the interesting birds and plant life we would see, but didn't. The sky remained grey but

did not spit at us. Dad tried to keep our spirits up by mar-
velling at the wonderful surroundings. He pointed out a
plant that looked like a clump of grass with black spears
sticking up at the middle. It wasn't in the pamphlet, so
he didn't know what it was called. Nevertheless it was
interesting. *Everything* was interesting, he assured us.

Then he was bitten by a bullant that had somehow
crawled up his leg. Mum was determined to take him
back to the caravan park and apply antiseptic cream.
She reminded Dad that she had wanted to put antiseptic
cream in her backpack, but he had said not to bother.
Dad said that Mum wasn't helping matters by being
smug. Even though they had to go back (by now, Dad
had to lean on Mum to walk), I wanted to keep walking with Briony. Mum was reluctant, but I promised to
keep to the track, and be back in less than an hour. They
could rely on me. I was twelve, old enough to set a good
example for my sister. Briony sensibly asked Dad and
Mum if we could have their chocolate bars and trail mix.

The path descended steeply into a gully. The air was
cooler and the vegetation changed. There were big ferns
and sprays of bracken. There were fewer bird noises.
Briony and I came to a signpost at a fork in the path. If
we took the left path we could continue along the old
Pichi Richi Pass nature trail. If we went to the right, we
would be taking the *new* Pichi Richi Pass nature trail.
We decided it was time to go back.

Then I noticed something about the sign. If you take
away the first letter of the three words in Pichi Richi
Pass you get Ichi Ichi Ass. I told Briony this and she

nearly wet herself laughing. This was an even better joke than the one about the elegant lady soiling herself at the health spa. Somehow, I had to alter the sign, so that others would see the brilliant joke. The sign was too high for me to reach. I needed to stand on something. I told Briony to wait by the sign and went in search of something to stand on.

I found a log that smelled sweet with rot. When I lifted it, hundreds of cockroaches streamed out from underneath. I gasped and let go of the log. Cockroaches ran up my arms. I tried to brush them off. Did cockroaches bite? Were they poisonous? I kept slapping at the red bugs until the last one had fallen. Then I kicked hard at the log, to teach the cockroaches that I was the boss. The log was mine. I was the overlord and they weren't going to stop me taking what I wanted. Waves of cockroaches fled from the log that had been their home. Then I dragged the log to the track where I had left Briony.

Just as I reached the track, the light in the forest seemed to dim and a single cockroach crawled out of the log. Unlike the others, this one wasn't afraid. It was as large as my palm. I froze. With its feelers vibrating, the giant cockroach crawled towards my hands. I could see myself reflected in its eyes. I was a frightened little kid, not an overlord. This cockroach wanted me to know that I *wasn't* the boss. It knew I was scared. It knew that it could kill me if it wanted, that it had a deadly sting. Once it had made this clear, it crawled back into the log.

The forest grew lighter, as if the cockroach had brought with it a host of shadows.

I was on the track, in front of the sign, but Briony had gone.

'Briony? Where are you, Briony?'

There was no answer. Soon my voice was hoarse from calling. All I heard was the forest with its new, unwelcoming sounds. I had lost Briony. Somehow I would have to explain this to Mum and Dad.

I had lost my sister.

CHAPTER 3

Len's snoring is louder and more disgusting than ever. I climb out of bed, leave the room and go for a midnight walk.

I like it when the night-lights are on and the corridors are empty. There are nurses on duty, but they're watching television in the nurses' station. I slip by without them noticing. I don't mean to be harsh on the nurses. They have a tough job. They are sometimes sworn at and threatened. A patient who had too much anger in him even hit Keith, the nurse with the beard. (Dr Parkinson got into trouble about that.) But the nurses keep coming to work. Either they care about us, or they're very good actors.

I want to see where Anthea sleeps. As I walk I try *very* hard not to see the shiny guys. Since Grace the druggie has gone, it makes sense that Anthea will be in the bed she vacated. The trouble is, I can't remember which bed was Grace's.

Unlike Mango, I don't find Anthea beautiful. I don't find anyone beautiful, except for characters in books – and I read science fiction. But Anthea is frail. She looks as though a harsh word could kill her. I screwed up by talking to her about the shiny guys. I'm going to make amends by looking out for her and making sure that she is protected. If she's sharing a room with a klepto like me, I'll tell her that Tim is the nurse to whom she should entrust her valuables. If she's with a drug thief, I'll make sure that she doesn't take her eyes off the cup the nurses give to her. Some of the drug thieves can do magic, just as I can. They palm tablets the way I palm coins.

I hear nasal noises of varying pitch as I walk the corridors.

There's a fluttering shape at the edge of my peripheral vision. If I concentrate I can make him go away. I stand still and think of a good moment in my life, before the shiny guys turned up. I think of primary school and Briony and how we made each other laugh by having what we called 'water tastings'. People thought it strange that Briony and I played together at school. It was unusual for a brother and sister. But Briony was so good at making me laugh; I loved her to bits.

Not far from the shelter sheds there was a row of twelve bubblers, or 'drinking fountains' as we were supposed to call them. Briony and I would work our way along the bubblers, sampling each one, sloshing the water in our mouths then spitting it out. Like wine judges we then pronounced what the water tasted like.

We weren't allowed to say it tasted like pee or other dis-gusting things until we got to the last few taps. That always made us laugh so much, we had to stop play-ing. Briony invented the game. She probably saw wine judging on TV. 'This water has a strong carroty taste. It would go very well with a meal of human hair and lawn clippings.' 'This water tastes like strawberry and would be best served with curried chicken bums.' Briony was always better at the descriptions than I was. If she came up with a really good one while I was still sloshing water in my mouth, I would burst out laughing and spray water everywhere.

That was a good time, back when the worst thing that could happen to you was wetting your pants in class after a long water-tasting session.

The shiny guy has gone. I resume my investigation.

Anthea is sharing a room with alcoholic Val. They sleep in the half-light. Val has decorated the wall behind her bed as though she intends to spend some time here. There are posters of religious stuff. There's even one of those three dimensional pictures of Jesus where his heart floats in front of him, as if he's doing a magic trick. Val has put up religious posters because she goes to Alcoholics Anonymous, and they reckon that the only way to get off the booze is to believe in a higher power. She tells us every day about how she is an alcoholic but God is keeping her well. I feel sorry for Anthea. Imagine having to share a room with a boring alcoholic. I suppose it could be worse.

I was wrong. Anthea *is* good-looking, even though

she is very thin. Her hair has been washed. It's shiny and straight and lies over the pillow in a way that makes it look like a photographer spent ages getting it just right. I like the way her eyes are far apart like a beautiful alien from a science-fiction novel. Anthea looks peaceful. Maybe she's lucky and the shiny guys don't haunt her sleep as they do mine. Someone has brought her flowers, so she is obviously loved.

Val received flowers once. They looked like they'd been bought from a bucket at a roadside stall, but Val was proud and asked the nurses for a vase. She was desperate for the flowers not to die and started putting aspirins in the water, which is supposed to make them last longer. When she ran out of aspirins, she hoarded her tablets and dropped them in the vase. Val was turning her flowers into drug addicts. In the end one of the cleaners took them away without Val knowing. She was very upset. But I told her not to worry. Her flowers were probably in rehab.

I move out of the Jesus room, leaving its occupants to their dreams. I'm glad I saw Anthea. It's difficult for anyone in Ward 44 to look peaceful and dignified, but that's how she looked.

I stop outside Mango's room. He shares with John, the quiet Korean kid. Because of his attachment disorder, Mango sometimes grabs hold of John. John doesn't complain. He hardly ever says anything. I don't know why he's in the hospital. We have ward meetings once a week, where everyone is supposed to tell some positive news. John doesn't say a word. He's sleeping soundly tonight. But Mango's bed is empty. I am not the only nocturnal wanderer.

I creep past the nurses' station. Shamita and Keith are still watching television. Keith is short and stocky. His arms are almost as big as Mango's. He's the nurse they summon when there's heavy lifting to be done. He's a smoker and you can smell it on him from metres away. He's the only nurse who isn't determinedly nice, but that's understandable, since he was hit by the patient with too much anger.

There is the fluttering shape again, over to the right, just beyond what I can easily see. The shiny guys are busy tonight. I won't turn my head. If I do, all that will happen is they'll disappear from my direct view and relocate to the periphery. They'll keep jumping around and if I try to follow them with my eyes I might pass out. It's happened before. Instead I'll think of good times with Briony. That'll make the shiny guys disappear.

I am grabbed from behind.

'Mental case,' I whisper.

'Spazzo,' whispers Mango.

'When are you going to let me go?'

'I don't know. In a minute.'

Mango takes deep, slow breaths.

'Mango, are you sure you don't get a sexual kick out of this?'

'I told you already. No.'

'Then why do you do it?'

'I don't know.'

'It's not normal.'

'That's why I'm here.'

'How come you're breathing slow like that?'

'Dr Patel said it might help me to let go.'

'Do you prefer doing it to girls or boys?'

'I'd prefer not do it to anyone.'

Mango is being honest, even though his affliction seems unbelievable. He hugs indiscriminately. He doesn't know why he does it. He doesn't *want* to do it. But he can't help himself. It sounds like a fake illness that a pervert would invent.

'I'm glad you came along,' I say. 'One of the shiny guys was over there.'

'Really?'

'Yes, but he's gone now. How long have you been awake?'

'A couple of hours.'

'What have you been doing?'

'I went to look at Anthea.'

'Jesus, Mango, what if you'd grabbed her? Worse still, you might have grabbed alcoholic Val. That would have been a catastrophe.'

Mango laughs softly. 'I like the way you talk. I've never met anyone who talks like you do. At first I thought you were putting it on. I didn't like you.'

'I didn't like you either.'

'Why not?'

'I thought you might bash me up. I sometimes get bashed up at school.'

'Because of the way you talk?'

'Yes.'

'If I was there, no one would bash you up.'

'If they saw us like this, they'd probably kill us.'

'They could try. I'll let you go in a minute.'

'I know. It's okay.'

Mango tries some more slow breathing.

'Do you think the impossible cupboard is real?' he asks.

'Yes.'

'Seriously?'

'Undoubtedly.'

'Yeah. It's out there somewhere. If I could just find it . . . and destroy it . . . I reckon my whole life would change.'

Mango lets me go. It isn't a gradual thing. He just drops his grip. Something in his brain tells him that he no longer needs to do what he's been doing for the last few minutes. We face each other and continue the conversation as if nothing happened.

'When we get out, I'll help you find it,' I say.

'And I'll help you to kill the shiny guys,' says Mango.

It's the same pact we always make.

'Good night, spazzo,' says Mango.

'Good night, mental case.'

CHAPTER 4

I hait th imposible cubbard. Wat I hait most is I dont understan why it freeks me so mch.

I am traped in a cubbard. It is v dark. I try to yel out but no sound com out my mouth. The dors wont open.

The dors dont mak sens becos ther is one at the front of the cubbard and one at the bak of the cubbard. I hav never sen a cubbard lik this befor. It is not v deep. There is hadly enuough room for me and that was wen I was thin. The werd thing is ther are two dornobs insid. One of the dornobs is on the front of the cubbard and one of the dornobs is on the bak of the cubbard. It is v strange.

I dont understan why a cubbard is made lik this only that it is the wost place in the world and I hait to be loked in. That is th dream I all ways hav and I hait it. I think if I cood fin that cubbard th dreams mit stop even tho docter partel say this mite not werk. He even think

I cood be gay becos some gay peeple ar stuk in cubbards but he is v rong about that.

It is embrassing to be freeked by a cubbard. Kolin has montsers. But I wood preferr th montsers to the cubbard.

CHAPTER 5

The real estate agent's name was Andrew. He was convinced that our house would fetch a high price, provided we made it look special for the inspections. We had to clean all windows thoroughly, and open them to let in air. Andrew mentioned that it was vital to air out the bedrooms of teenage boys. I was twelve at the time, but I was offended on behalf of the teenager I would become.

Andrew arrived ten minutes before the inspection. He explained it would be best for us to leave. Customers don't feel comfortable when the occupants of the house are on the premises. Dad asked Andrew if he could prevent people from entering the front bedroom upstairs, the loft where Briony used to sleep. Andrew told us he couldn't do that. He would be downstairs handing out leaflets and answering questions from potential purchasers. It would be a mistake to turn customers away from one room. They might think there was something wrong with it. Maybe it had a ghost. Mum asked if

Andrew could tell his clients to be very *careful* in the room. Andrew said he would try his best, but we knew his word wasn't enough.

'We prefer to stay during the inspection,' said Dad. 'We'll sit in the loft and gaze out of the window. We won't look at the customers and make them feel embarrassed.'

'I really wouldn't recommend that, Mr Lapsley,' said Andrew.

'Nevertheless it's what we'd like to do,' said Dad.

Andrew adjusted his tie and went outside to put up the 'For Inspection' flag.

In silence, Mum, Dad and I sat on Briony's bed. Dad sat in the middle. Mum held his hand. This prompted Dad to hold my hand as well, something he rarely did.

'We should never have left you,' said Dad.

'Please don't start this,' I said.

'We should never have left you and Briony in that forest. What were we thinking?'

We'd been having this conversation for the past three months. Mum and Dad said they would never forgive themselves for abandoning Briony and me. But we hadn't been abandoned. The national park was a safe place, with paths and signs and other hikers. I knew not to talk to strangers, even if they were hikers who looked just like us.

'I wandered off the path,' I said.

'Not far, Colin. Not far at all.' Mum blew her nose as the tears came. 'It wasn't your fault. It was ours.'

What we all wanted to know was: why couldn't the police find Briony? And why didn't they start looking as soon as we reported her missing? If they'd started earlier they might have found her. But police procedure doesn't work like that. Briony had been gone for only an hour when we contacted them, and that was too soon. Kids were always wandering off, they told us. There had been no suspicious circumstances. I hadn't seen anyone lurking. We were told to contact the police if Briony didn't return within the next two hours. Frantic with worry, Dad, Mum and I searched on our own. Two hours later, we called the police again. They agreed that now was the time to launch an official search. Later they told us that we shouldn't have trampled all over the place where Briony had disappeared. It made it difficult to find clues. Did they really expect us not to go searching?

Holding hands on Briony's bed we stopped our daily ritual of self-blame. After all, the inspection was about to start. Mum dried her tears, because she knew that no one would buy a house with a crying lady in it. We didn't speak as prospective buyers arrived. They didn't stay long in Briony's room. We had our backs to them, so we didn't see their expressions. A kid made a racist comment about Briony's *Monkey* posters. (Briony once had a crush on Masaaki Sakai, the handsome actor who played Monkey in the Japanese television series.) A lady remarked to her friend that she liked the cactus on the windowsill. It grew in a pot that Briony made at school.

Half an hour later the inspection was over. Through the open window we overheard Andrew talking to a prospective buyer on the front landing directly below. We were desperate to sell, he told the buyer, because there had been a tragedy in the family. A little girl had gone missing a few months ago. Dad had asked Andrew not to mention this. Andrew went on to reassure the customer that the incident had occurred in a state forest in South Australia, not in the local area, which was family friendly and handy for the shops. Andrew didn't say much else because Dad picked up Briony's cactus and dropped it out of the window and on his head. It wasn't a big potted cactus. Andrew survived and did not press charges. We sold the house at auction. I don't know if we got a good price or not. I just remember how angry Mum was with Dad for dropping the potted cactus onto the estate agent, though she forgave him when she realised the pot had not been broken.

CHAPTER 6

Len has disappeared. The staff are nervous, though trying to hide it. It is bad that Len has somehow managed to leave the hospital without anyone knowing. Since Len and I share a bedroom, and since I was the last person to see him, Dr Parkinson is eager to talk with me. He tries to maintain his usual measured demeanour but I sense that he's agitated.

'Did Len mention that he was going to leave the hospital?' Dr Parkinson asks.

I shake my head. 'Len and I don't speak that often. You should have a word with Val. Those two were always talking.'

'We've already spoken with her.'

'What did she say? I bet it was something about God. Then she flattered you about your hair.'

Dr Parkinson ignores my snide remarks.

'Last night, did Len seem different in any way?'

'He stank; he was horrible and ugly. No, he didn't

seem any different.'

'Colin . . .'

'I'm just telling the truth.'

Dr Parkinson rubs his chin. He wants to reprimand me, but he still needs my help, so he reconsiders.

'What time did you go to sleep?' he says.

'About nine o'clock.'

'And Len was in his bed?'

'Yes. Then I woke up at midnight.'

'And Len was still in the other bed?'

'Definitely. His snoring woke me up.'

'Did you fall asleep again? Or were you awake for a while?'

'I was awake for a while.'

'And Len was still snoring? He was there the whole time you were awake?'

'I'm not really sure.'

Dr Parkinson regards me with forensic interest. 'Not sure?'

'I left the room. I needed to go to the toilet.'

'And when you came back he was still there?'

'I didn't go straight back to the room.'

'Where did you go?'

'I . . . um . . . had a walk.'

'Where?'

'Just around the ward. I thought it might help me get back to sleep.'

'Shamita and Keith didn't see you?'

'I didn't want to bother anyone.'

'If you were suffering from insomnia, they would

have been able to help.'

'I don't want to take too many drugs.'

'How long was it before you returned to your room?'

'Probably about two hours.'

Dr Parkinson is perfectly still, unblinking. I've seen him do this before, when I've said something that doesn't seem correct.

'Two hours?'

'It was a long walk.'

'Do you often take long walks at night?'

'Not often.'

'I'd like you to stop doing it.'

'Okay.'

'What happened next?'

'I got back from my walk. It was two.'

'And when you got to your room – was Len still there?'

'I really don't know. If he was, he wasn't snoring.'

'So, he might not have been there? He might have walked away in the two hours that you weren't in the room?'

I surprise myself by making a brilliant deduction. 'He didn't leave,' I say. 'Not by choice, anyway.'

'What do you mean?'

'When I woke up this morning, Len wasn't there but his basket was. If he planned on leaving, he would have taken the basket. It's his favourite thing in the world. Are you sure he's not hiding somewhere? Don't you have surveillance cameras?'

Dr Parkinson shakes his head. 'I've always considered them intrusive. This isn't *1984*.'

I nod. 'That was last year.'

'I was talking about the book.'

'I know that, Dr Parkinson.'

'Of course. Of course you know.' Dr Parkinson looks irritated, but returns to his point. 'If a patient sees a surveillance camera, what's he going to think?'

'Well, that he's being surveilled.'

'And would you feel comfortable with that? To know you were always being watched? Would that help you to get well?'

'Probably not.'

'Exactly.'

'I'm not sure the basket-weaving helps either,' I say.

Dr Parkinson frowns. 'That's the army's fault.'

I must look bewildered because Dr Parkinson feels the need to explain that Ward 44 used to be part of a repatriation hospital.

'The army was always big on basket-weaving,' Dr Parkinson says. 'I spent two years on that board trying to get a proper arts-and-crafts workshop. In the end they gave me an old storeroom full of asbestos.'

It's obviously a touchy subject. 'I don't mind the basket-weaving that much,' I say.

'It's an interim measure.'

'Was this always a psychiatric ward?'

'Oh yes. We still admit some Vietnam vets.'

'Don't Vietnamese peasants wear hats woven from bamboo?'

'Yes, they do.'

'And the soldiers would have been frightened of the

peasants because they might have been the Viet Cong, even though they weren't wearing uniforms or helmets?'

'That's right.'

'They were just wearing those cute hats that look like baskets.'

'Yes.'

'And the soldiers were sent to this ward so they could get over the horrible things they had seen and done.'

'Some still have terrible flashbacks.'

'Don't you think it's in really bad taste to have shell-shocked Vietnam vets weaving things that look like the hats worn by the people who were trying to kill them?'

'You know, I never thought of that irony.'

'I guess the army didn't either.'

'No.'

Dr Parkinson looks sad. I actually feel sorry for him and try to cheer him up.

'Watch this.' I make a nice little conjuring move with my hands. I reach for a coin, make it disappear then lean forward and produce it from Dr Parkinson's nose.

'Very good,' he says, not unkindly.

'You'd probably like the trick more if I made Len come out of your nose. That's harder.'

Dr Parkinson allows himself a little smile.

'Colin, you seem to have established good relations with most of the patients. The only one who has complained about you is Len. He said you don't leave him alone in the night.'

'Sometimes I pull his toe to stop him snoring. You'd do the same, Dr Parkinson, believe me. He sounds revolting when he snores. I'd rather sleep on the pool table.'

'And you swear you don't know anything about his disappearance?'

'I swear.'

'Thank you, Colin, that's all.'

'Can I stop taking the blue pills? They knock me around too much. And how come I'm on blue pills when nobody else is?'

'They're an anti-hallucinogen. They may help to get rid of your . . . "shiny guys". The medication has proved effective on patients suffering LSD flashbacks. Have you taken a lot of LSD in your life, Colin?'

I laugh. 'You can be funny, Dr Parkinson.'

'From you, I take that as high praise.'

'Do you ever wonder if I might be seeing what's actually there?'

'Shiny red men?'

'Wouldn't it be funny if they were real? What if I were the sane one and everyone else was mad?'

'Do you really believe that?'

'No.'

'Do you feel as though you're improving?'

'How do you mean?'

'Do you feel better than you did yesterday?'

'Not really.'

'But you do feel better than when you were first admitted?'

'I can't remember how I felt then. That was four weeks ago. Isn't that a long time to be in a psychiatric ward?'

'Not at all. In Ward 44 the average is eight weeks.'

'I won't be here that long.'

'I won't discharge you until I'm convinced that we have found a way to treat your depression.'

Dr Parkinson rubs his eyes.

'It must be hard to run a place like this and be a psychiatrist as well,' I say.

'I enjoy the challenge.'

'But don't you make mistakes? When you've got so much to think about?'

'If you'd prefer to see another psychiatrist –'

'No, that's okay. I don't think they'd be much help either.'

'We'll try something else.'

Anthea and alcoholic Val are sitting on a bench in the courtyard garden. I look through the window of the dining room, unsure if I should interrupt. Poor Anthea is being talked at by Val. It would be obvious to everyone except Val that Anthea is not enjoying the conversation, even though it's bound to be peppered with compliments.

I'm filling in my meal card. I have to decide now what I would like to eat tomorrow for breakfast, lunch and dinner. It seems a huge task to prepare so far ahead. Will I really feel like roast chicken for dinner tomorrow night, or will I prefer the beef? I decide to be impulsive. I tick the vegetarian meal, even though I'm not a vegetarian. The vegetarians have a rough time here. While the carnivores are told exactly what to expect for dinner, the vegetarians are given no clue whatever. All it says on the card is 'vegetarian meal'. It might be just a capsicum stuffed with another capsicum, or a vegetarian lasagne so perfect that it makes the carnivores jealous. Every now and then I *like* that level of uncertainty in my life, and I become an honorary vegetarian for a day.

There are slices of fruitcake laid out on the counter, but we are not supposed to eat them until morning tea.

'Hello, spazzo.'

'Hello, mental case.'

Mango has grabbed two pieces of fruitcake. He insists I have the big one because I'm too skinny. I tell him I'm not hungry. Mango will have to eat both slices or he will have to put one back. It doesn't take him long to reach a decision. We sit together and fill in our meal cards. Mango ticks every box as he chews on the cake. It says clearly that patients should tick only *one* of the three boxes, but that doesn't stop him. Mango never receives all the meals, but someone is getting the message because his serves are always large.

'Do you think Len ran away?'

I shake my head. 'He left his basket behind. He'd never do that if he ran away.'

'He loves the basket that much?'

'It's almost sexual.'

'Tick the ice-cream twice,' says Mango, pointing at my card.

'I don't like ice-cream. Why would I want it twice?'

'You need it.'

'No one needs it.'

'I'll eat it.'

I double-tick the ice-cream.

We look at Anthea and Val sharing the bench in the morning sunshine.

'She's beautiful,' says Mango.

'Alcoholic Val?'

'Shut up.'

Then the fluttering shape appears. This time it's off to my left. One of the shiny guys is not far away. Stupidly, I look to my left and the shiny guy leaps out of view. He's still there, behind me. But I won't turn around because that's what he wants.

'You can see one, can't you?' says Mango.

'He's behind me.'

Mango scours the room. 'I don't see anyone.'

'You're lucky.'

In the courtyard, Anthea flinches and looks in my direction.

'She's looking at you,' says Mango.

'No, she isn't,' I say.

'She's looking straight at you.'

I nod slowly as realisation dawns. 'She can see what's behind me.'

'The shiny guy?'

'That's what she's looking at.'

Anthea goes back to studying her slippers while Val babbles on, probably telling uplifting biblical stories about plagues of frogs and water turning to blood.

'Go and talk to her,' says Mango.

A nurse approaches Anthea and she is led away.

CHAPTER 7

Q. Do you know where you are, Anthea?

A. Another hospital.

Q. Do you know why?

A. Food poisoning.

Q. That isn't why they pumped your stomach.

A. I ate a bad prawn.

Q. Anthea, you haven't eaten in days.

A. I'm on a diet.

Q. You are thin. Some would say too thin. I'd like you to eat during your stay with us. The food here is fine.

A. Okay.

Q. You say it as though you don't mean it. The staff know about anorexia. They will be looking out for your best interests. They will make sure you eat and they will tell me if you go to the toilet to vomit.

A. Okay.

Q. In the end, they didn't need to pump your stomach. But they thought you'd taken pills.

A. It was speed.

Q. Was it the first time you've taken speed?

A. Yes.

Q. Are you sure?

A. There may have been a few other times.

Q. How many?

A. About ten thousand.

Q. Please, be serious.

A. Okay, I started taking it a year ago, and only on the weekend.

Q. Where do you get it?

A. Do you want some?

Q. Anthea –

A. If you're a doctor, can't you just write yourself a prescription?

Q. We can stop if you want.

A. I got it from kids at school. Then from my ex-boyfriend.

Q. Did speed ever make you sick before?

A. No. It made me feel good, like I wasn't me.

Q. You don't like being you?

A. Wow. Good guess.

Q. . . .

A. Yes, I don't like being me. I'd rather be Carla.

Q. Who is she?

A. My sister. She's beautiful.

Q. You are also attractive.

A. She's normal.

Q. And you're not normal?

A. Sometimes I see shadows that aren't there.

Q. Tell me about them.

A. I feel stupid.

Q. You're not stupid. Please tell me about the shadows.

A. They follow me. Especially when I'm sad. Which is most of the time.

Q. Can you remember when you first saw them?

A. I've always seen them.

Q. Did you tell anyone?

A. Mum said I was making them up. So I stopped telling people.

Q. When you take speed . . . do you see the shadows?

A. Never. They disappear.

Q. That must be a relief.

A. It is.

Q. But they come back?

A. Yes.

Q. Worse than before? After the speed wears off?

A. Sometimes. Yes.

Q. Does Carla know you take speed?

A. No. I told you, she's perfect.

Q. Nobody's perfect.

A. She is.

Q. Do you resent her?

A. Oh, shut up.

Q. Is that such a bad question?

A. Just a very predictable one. I've spoken with psychologists before.

Q. I'm a psychiatrist.

A. I'll make your job easy. Do you know what my problem is?

Q. Tell me what you think it is.

A. I'm stupid. That's all.

Q. I'm sure you're not.

A. This isn't a normal hospital is it?

Q. What makes you say that?

A. The grey pyjamas are a bit of a giveaway.

Q. They are Dr Parkinson's idea. He's in charge of the ward.

A. Why do we wear them?

Q. Why do you think?

A. So we're all equal?

Q. See? You're not stupid at all.

CHAPTER 8

Dad read from the card.

'What is the most common element in the universe?'

'Hydrogen,' I said.

'That's too easy,' Dad said.

'*I* didn't know that hydrogen was the most common element in the universe,' Mum said.

'What did you think it was?' said Dad. 'Sultanas? Do you think the rings around Saturn are made of sultanas?'

I liked it when Mum and Dad bickered like this. It made Trivial Pursuit a more interesting game. When Mum and Dad cottoned on that I enjoyed their arguments, they went to extra effort to make them funny. If they worried that I wasn't bringing home friends from school and was happy to play Trivial Pursuit with them, they never said anything. It had taken us three years to be happy together again; three years since we had moved into the new house. And a little over three years since Briony disappeared. It was hard to believe. She had been out of our lives for that long and we were just beginning to play games and smile a little. We still grieved, but we did it individually, not with one another. Grief and joy had their separate spaces, just like the little coloured segments that went into a Trivial Pursuit counter.

'I've had three science questions so far and they've all been impossible,' Dad complained. *'What is the largest organ of the human body?* That's a trick question.'

'It's the skin. Everyone knows that,' Mum said.

'How do we know? Have you seen anyone's skin in a bundle? How do we know the lungs aren't bigger?'

'Because it says so on the card.'

'But lungs are huge. And what about the larger intestine? That goes on for miles. You can't tell me that the larger intestine isn't bigger than the human skin. I read that some of these cards are wrong.' We'd heard this argument before. 'I'm pretty sure that one about the Taj Mahal is wrong. It's definitely in Bombay.'

'Agra,' Mum said, shaking her head. 'And it's the Taj Mahal that planes are forbidden to fly over. Not cows.'

We were startled when the doorbell rang, because we didn't receive many visitors. The police officer had a quiet formal manner and brought terrible news. He wanted us to hear it from a human being, he said, not the television. He didn't stay long but added that we would be contacted again. Counselling would be provided, he told us. And he was very sorry.

The police believed they had found Briony's body, along with the other kids'. Hearing it opened up old wounds. It was as if we had lost her all over again.

Moving to the new house had helped to bury some of the sorrow. Now it came bubbling back to the surface. The following morning, after a sleepless night, Mum and Dad rang to tell their bosses that they would not be working today. They didn't need to explain why. The news was already being broadcast.

That evening we received a visit from two more police officers. One barely spoke. The older one carried a Manilla folder and wanted to know if he could ask a few questions.

'I understand it's difficult,' he said, 'but there are one or two things we need to know.'

'Can't it wait?' Dad asked.

'It's urgent and may assist the investigation,' said the officer.

'If it's not too much trouble,' added his colleague. It seemed his job was to be polite.

We sat at the dining-room table. The older officer opened his folder, and took out black-and-white photographs. They were all of the same man. He directed his questions to me.

'Do you recognise this man?'

'No,' I said.

'Please, take your time.'

'. . . no.'

'Have a good look.'

'I've never seen him before.'

'You didn't see him on the day Briony disappeared?'

My mouth was dry. I was sweating and I felt my parents watching.

'No. This man wasn't there,' I said.

'Are you sure?'

'I'm sure.'

'Did you see *anyone*? When Briony disappeared?'

'No.'

'You don't have to be afraid.'

'If there was someone there, I would have said.'

'You're absolutely sure?'

Dad stood. 'That's enough. You're upsetting him.'

'I'm sorry,' said the police officer. 'But –'

'No, that's enough.'

The police officer nodded. 'We'll leave you in peace.'

'Thank you for your assistance,' said the younger officer, whose job it was to be polite.

They piled the photographs into the folder and left.

Even though Dad had stood up to the police officer, I knew that things had changed.

'If you'd seen someone at the scene of the crime, you would have said something, wouldn't you?' Mum asked.

'Of course he would have,' said Dad. 'What a stupid question.'

But things had definitely changed.

After rummaging through some drawers in the bathroom, Mum found the three-year-old bottle of Valium tablets. It was still half full. Dad had told Mum that the tablets weren't a good idea, that she might become addicted. But the bottle had survived the move from one house to the next. Perhaps Mum had intended to throw the pills away but had forgotten. Or maybe she knew we might need them again. Even my father, who couldn't face another night like the one before, swallowed a little yellow pill.

I had dreams about the photographs. Nightmares. What had made no sense before began to fall into place. Suddenly, I remembered. I *did* know the man in the photo. I had seen him the day Briony disappeared. So why didn't I tell my parents or the police about him?

That night, the shiny guys paid me their first visit. They didn't speak, but I knew what they were thinking. They wanted to know why I had lied about not recognising the man. They wanted to know why I was protecting him. I honestly couldn't tell them, even though I knew I *had* lied to the police officer. What other explanation could there be? The shiny guys hated me for betraying so many people. Worst of all, I had betrayed Briony.

I didn't deserve to live.

I went to the bathroom. As I reached for the bottle of pills, I wondered if there were enough to do the trick. Apparently there weren't, and that's how I ended up in Ward 44.

I don't remember much about my first few days. On their second visit my parents brought me a present from Grandma. She hadn't been told that I was in a psychiatric ward, only that I was in hospital because I wasn't well. I unwrapped the present. It was a box of liqueur chocolates. My grandma is forgetful. She doesn't remember that I've stopped eating chocolate because it makes me sick, or that this is the very same box of chocolates that

I gave her for her birthday ten months ago, only with different wrapping paper and well past its USE BY date.

'Please thank Gran for me,' I told my parents.

We sat in the dining room drinking lukewarm coffee. Mum ate a chocolate or two. The conversation was stilted. Mum mentioned a TV comedy show that she and Dad had enjoyed recently. There was a particularly funny moment where a man driving a car was stopped by two little kids wearing police uniforms. The man turned to his wife and said, 'Is it just me, or do police officers seem to be getting younger?'

I didn't laugh. 'Sorry, I don't understand the joke.'

'It probably makes more sense to older people,' Mum said. 'When you get older, you really do believe that police officers look far too young to be police officers.'

I recalled the police officer who had come to ask me about the photographs. He hadn't looked young. His eyes were ancient.

Alcoholic Val wandered in, looking for someone to flatter. She introduced herself to my parents and told them that I was polite and good-looking, and smart enough to be an air traffic controller. My parents looked confused. They didn't know that alcoholic Val says nice things about everyone. If Pol Pot, the butcher of Cambodia, ended up in our ward she would probably compliment him on his bubbly personality and twinkling eyes. Mum offered alcoholic Val a chocolate. She happily accepted, then made herself a cup of tepid tea.

As Mum, Dad and I tried to converse, alcoholic Val helped herself to more chocolates. She said that Mum and Dad were kind to bring such wonderful chocolates, and that they also dressed well and used a superior brand of shampoo. My parents had started to twig about alcoholic Val. Then Val startled us by sobbing. She pushed away the chocolates. She told my parents that they had done a terrible thing. They had given alcohol to an alcoholic. Why had they been so cruel? Mum realised that the chocolates had liqueur centres, and Val had eaten seven. If someone came to breathalyse her, she might be over the legal limit and unable to drive a car around the ward. Mum tried to reassure Val that the chocolates would have been cheap. It probably wasn't even real alcohol in them. But Val said she could tell it was.

'Then why did you eat seven of them?' I asked.

Val had no answer for that and waddled out of the dining room, drunk on chocolates. My parents looked at me as though I had said something mean, but all I'd done was try to make them feel less guilty about giving alcohol to an alcoholic.

'Val's a loony,' I said.

'You shouldn't use words like that,' Mum said.

'Seriously, she's a loony. I think she'll be stuck here forever.'

'Are there any other . . . young patients?' Dad asked, hoping that I wasn't sharing the ward with a gaggle of mature-age mental-cases.

'There's Mango.'

'We met him last time,' Mum said. 'He seemed quite old.'

'He's only two years older than I am,' I said.

'Seventeen?' Mum said. 'He's a man.'

'We look out for each other.'

'Well, that's wonderful,' Mum said.

But my parents were concerned. After all, the friendship with Mango wasn't one that could continue when I was recovered and able to leave the ward. That would be inappropriate. I'd have to find friends at school. *Normal* friends.

Dad looked at his watch. 'We're breaking the rules, you know. Visiting hours are over.'

Mum collected the dirty cups.

'Leave those,' I said. 'I'll do them. They prefer it that way.'

Dad told me to get well soon. Mum told me she didn't blame me for anything. She hugged me tightly, as if to prove that she really meant what she said. But it was like a mechanical hug from Mango. I knew that she didn't mean it.

CHAPTER 9

It's the day of Len's disappearance. Tim, the tall blond nurse, enters the dining room. 'Come with me, please,' he tells me.

'Is this about Len?' I ask. 'Do I have to talk to the police or something?'

'No, you don't have to talk to the police,' Tim reassures me.

I turn to Mango. 'Can you put in my meal card?'

'Sure.'

'Mango, where should you be?' Tim asks.

All Mango wants to do is look at Anthea in the courtyard.

'I don't know,' he says.

'Go to the nurses' station,' says Tim. 'They will know.'

Tim leads me along the covered walkway that goes from the old building where Ward 44 is located, to the new building next door. The doors at either side of the walkway are kept locked. They open with a special key-card that the staff members wear on lanyards, alongside their photo identification. No one knows, but I have stolen a spare keycard from the nurses' station. I figure it will come in handy one day. It's under my bed with two books I stole from Dr Parkinson's office, three magazines and a chocolate bar. Mango likes chocolate. Clothes I took from the property cupboard are also stashed there.

Patients in the new building seem more normal than patients in Ward 44. Most of them wear proper clothes, not grey pyjamas. They don't look haunted or frightened. And they don't flinch or yell out for no reason.

'How is *The Castle*?' Tim asks.

I have no idea what he is referring to.

'The Kafka novel,' Tim prompts.

I recall the book I borrowed from the ward library; *The Castle* by the Czech writer Franz Kafka. Tim is a reader, like me. He recommended it.

'It's interesting,' I say.

'How much have you read?'

'I'm about halfway through.'

I use the joker from my deck of cards as a bookmark. I never fold down the corner of a page. And since I don't need the joker for any of my card games or tricks, I figure he's about the best bookmark you could have.

'It's weird,' I say. 'I used to be a good reader, but now I'm finding it hard.'

'That's normal. Happens to a lot of patients. But you like the book?'

'Yes.'

'Wait till you get to the last sentence,' Tim says.

'What's so special about the last sentence?'

'It's a secret.'

After turning various corners and climbing far too many stairs we arrive at our destination. The door is open. I see a small office without a window. Whoever works here can't be very important. The office is so neat that it's hard to believe anyone actually *does* work here. There are two pieces of blank paper on the desk, nothing more. The man sitting at the desk does not look like a doctor. He is immaculately dressed in a brown suit that is well pressed. He wears a white shirt, starched collar and a black tie that shines even in the fluorescent green-grey light. He's probably around forty, but I've never been good at guessing people's ages. I even get my own age wrong. I'm fifteen, but sometimes I'm more and sometimes less.

Behind the man is a framed photograph of a Dutch landscape. It's probably supposed to show patients how much peace and beauty there is in the world, though to me it looks foreboding, as though a dyke is about to break and flood the place, or the stately windmills might grow legs and run around slicing up peasants with their sails.

To the left of the landscape is a door that is slightly ajar. Beyond it is a perfectly white room with a bed and a solitary machine that looks far too important for its own good. I recall the sketch from the last Monty Python movie and wonder if this could be the famous machine that goes *Ping!* It wasn't a great movie. There weren't enough gags and I couldn't watch when the two surgeons pulled the liver out of the man while he was still alive and crying out in agony. I'm squeamish like that. I've been known to pass out when I see something horrible. It's earned me a nickname: *Collapsley.* But I liked the machine that goes *Ping!* That was a good joke.

Tim closes the door and leaves. The man at the desk smiles and asks if I would like some water. He tells me his name is Dr Vendra. I tell him my name is Colin and that I don't need water. This seems to please Dr Vendra immensely, though I don't see why it should. He asks me to sit. When he speaks I detect a slight accent that I cannot place.

'Are you a psychiatrist?' I ask.

'No.'

'Are you from the police?'

'Heavens, no. Why do you keep looking at that picture?' he asks.

'Sorry. I didn't mean to be rude.'

Dr Vendra chuckles. 'It's not likely to happen, you know.'

'What isn't?'

'There probably won't be a flood and the windmills won't start killing people. You can relax.'

The thought that this prim-looking man is able to read my mind doesn't relax me in the least.

'And I can't read your mind,' he adds. 'So you have nothing to worry about. You don't appear to have sat down yet.'

I sit.

'Are you comfortable?'

'You tell me,' I say.

Dr Vendra ignores this remark. 'Colin, I wonder if you could turn over that first piece of paper on the desk.'

I turn it over.

'Can you tell me what you see?'

It's a picture of a cat – one of those cats that every kid can draw, made from the letters M, O and Q. M for the ears, O for the face and Q for the body.

M
O
Q

'I'm waiting, Colin.' Dr Vendra sounds playful, but he obviously wants an answer.

'It's a picture of a cat,' I say.

'It is indeed. How many tails does the cat have?'

I don't always trust doctors. 'Is this a trick question?'

Dr Vendra smiles. He's completely charming. 'It isn't a trick question. How many tails?'

'One tail,' I say. 'The cat has one tail.'

'Good. Very good. Now please turn over the second piece of paper.'

I turn it over. It's the MOQ cat again, except this time there is a second tail on the left, opposite the first.

'How many tails does *this* cat have?' asks Dr Vendra.

'I thought you were going to ask me questions about Len's disappearance.'

'How many tails, Colin?' This time he sounds a little petulant.

'Two,' I say.

'Are you sure?'

'Positive.'

'You're right. The cat does indeed have two tails,' he says. 'It may interest you to know that some people wouldn't see the second tail. They'd think it was a perfectly normal cat. If I asked them to copy it, they would draw a cat with one tail.'

It sounds like nonsense. 'Why?'

'An excellent question.' Dr Vendra is delighted that I've asked what any normal person would ask. 'The answer is, a person who doesn't see the second tail is suffering from something called *sensory neglect*.'

'But I can see it,' I say.

'Indeed you can.'

'So I am not suffering from sensory neglect.'

'This would appear to be the case.'

'There's a book about it in the library in Ward 44.'

'I'd be surprised.'

'But I've read something, just recently.'

'Then you are being given the wrong books. You haven't been stealing from Dr Parkinson, have you?'

I pause. 'Dr Vendra, I don't understand what this is about.'

'Most people aren't getting the full picture. But you, Colin, can see that the cat actually has *three* tails.'

I look at the picture. The cat does not magically grow a third tail.

'I'm sorry. The cat definitely has two tails.'

'Look away at the wall, then back at the piece of paper.'

I do as asked. For a fraction of a second, there does

appear to be a third tail on the cat.

'How did that happen?' I ask.

'Interesting, isn't it?'

'You have a nice accent,' I say.

'Thank you.'

'Where are you from?'

'Nestor,' says Dr Vendra.

'Is that in Eastern Europe?'

'Quite possibly. Let's try something else.'

His eyes are intense but welcoming. I can't help but like Dr Vendra. He holds up three fingers on his left hand.

'How many fingers do you see?'

'Three,' I say.

'Correct.' He puts down his hand and raises it again. 'Now, how many fingers am I holding up? And please let's have no nonsense about the thumb not being a finger. For the purposes of this demonstration it is.'

'In that case you are holding up five fingers.'

'Splendid. Your answers are clear and concise.'

'They're not exactly hard questions.'

'Colin, I don't want you to take your eyes off mine. Can you do that for me?'

I look into Dr Vendra's sharp eyes and nod. 'I'm sure I can manage that,' I say.

'Without looking away, tell me how many fingers I'm holding up.'

Dr Vendra holds his arm out. Instinctively my eyes follow it. He drops his arm to his side.

'Eyes on mine, Colin.'

'Sorry.'

I lock eyes with Dr Vendra. He holds out his arm again.

'How many fingers am I holding up?'

'You're holding them all up,' I say.

'I want you to tell me how many there are. Don't look.'

I see it for a moment; the impossible thing that Dr Vendra wants me to see.

'You have six fingers,' I whisper.

'How many?'

'Six. Well, five now. But when I was looking into your eyes –'

'I had six fingers.'

'Yes.'

'You're sure?'

'I suppose that makes me crazy.'

'Not at all. I'm going to ask you to do me a huge favour. I want you to walk through the third doorway with me.'

There are only two doorways in the room, the one next to the framed landscape and the one through which I entered.

'There is no third doorway,' I say.

'I think you'll find there is. Look again.'

Dr Vendra points to the far corner of the room. Sure enough, there is a doorway there. I didn't notice it before. It's unlike me not to notice a whole doorway. I may be disoriented after the confusing journey with Tim, but I believe this doorway is on the outer wall of the building.

Unless there is a balcony on the other side of that door, Dr Vendra and I will walk into air and plummet to the ground.

'Would you be prepared to walk through the third doorway with me?' Dr Vendra asks.

I nod. 'I would.'

Dr Vendra stands. 'After you,' he says, pushing the door ajar. There is a dim yellow light beyond it. Dr Vendra sees my reluctance. 'You must go first, Colin. I have to hold the door open for you. It's hot and you might get burned.'

'And you won't?'

'My hands are different from yours. You may ask one final question.'

I don't hesitate. 'Where are we going?'

'Nestor,' says Dr Vendra.

Dr Vendra rests his free hand on my shoulder. If this is supposed to give me confidence, it doesn't. I see the hand resting on my shoulder, but I don't feel it. The hand has no substance. It looks solid but it might as well be made of mist.

Dr Vendra takes his hand away and smiles.

'Do you still want to do it?'

I feel a sharp pricking sensation in my upper arm as I walk through the doorway.

CHAPTER 10

'Welcome to the third tail of the cat,' says Dr Vendra grandly.

The surroundings have changed impossibly. Behind me, the doorway turns to dust. I'm standing in a desolate landscape. A vast foggy plain reaches out to an invisible horizon. Lone towers of rock are dotted here and there. As my eyes adjust to the peculiar light, I see that the towers are buildings. They don't have sharp edges, like normal buildings, the ones that exist on an earth that I've surely left. Either they are roughly made or they are once linear buildings that have deteriorated. Dr Vendra supports me by the shoulder. His hands are now solid, capable of bearing loads and applying pressure. If this is Nestor, I doubt very much that it's in Eastern Europe.

'Have I been drugged?' I ask.

'You're hyperventilating. I'll get you a paper bag to breathe into.'

Dr Vendra looks and sounds the same as he did

back in the office, though the surplus of fingers is now obvious.

'My arm hurts a bit. Did someone give me an injection?'

'Why would we do that?'

'Did you put drugs in my water?' I ask.

'You didn't drink water. I offered, but you said no.'

'I would have said yes if I'd known I was coming here. How far have I travelled?'

'From one door to the next? About thirty centimetres. Dimensionally is another matter.'

I can make out smaller shapes between the tall buildings. They are vaguely geometrical, though these shapes also lack the linear contours. The fog begins to lift and I see that the shapes are not randomly spaced. They are arranged in a series of grids. I'm looking at a city, or perhaps the remains of one, since there is no sign of life.

'I'm feeling better,' I say. 'I won't need the paper bag.'

'Splendid.'

'I don't see any trees.'

'We don't have any. Not in this neck of the woods, anyway.'

'Then how do you make paper bags? And how can I feel you holding me when I couldn't before?'

'Which is the more important question?' asks Dr Vendra.

'Probably the second one.'

'I'll try to explain. We have a little way to walk. Can I let you go? You won't fall over?'

'I'll be fine.'

Dr Vendra backs away gently. When he sees that I can stand upright unassisted, he paces forth.

'Please follow me.'

The yellow light from an invisible sun is like a sodium street lamp warming up. My vision continues to improve. We are on an outdoor concourse. It could be a bridge, though I'm too far from the edge to be certain. It's empty. Can we really be the only people in this place?

'Please, Colin. Do keep up.'

'Sure, Dr Vendra. Sorry.'

He walks swiftly towards a tall building. There are no sharp lines and there's no symmetry. Yet, at some stage there must have been. The structure's ungainly tilt must surely be accidental, not designed.

'You asked how it is that I am able to make tactile contact with you,' Dr Vendra says. He's too likeable to sound pompous.

'I also asked how you make paper bags, but you can ignore that question if you like.'

'I was born here, raised here and belong here,' Dr Vendra says. 'Since it's my world, I am afforded all the benefits of an inhabitant.'

'Do many humans come here?'

'Not voluntarily, no.' Dr Vendra checks himself. 'I probably shouldn't have said that. Forget I mentioned it.'

The building is huge but decrepit, as if it would collapse in a heavy wind.

'I must say you are making a fine fist of your introduction to Nestor,' Dr Vendra says. 'You seem almost calm.'

'I suppose I am. It may be the medication.'

'If I were you, I'd stop taking it.'

'Do you think?'

'I suspect you are calm for another reason.'

'Well I think it's because . . . what I'm experiencing means I'm *right*. I suppose I should be frightened, but I'm not. And . . . I'm about to see some red shiny guys, aren't I?'

Dr Vendra chuckles. 'Yes, Colin. You may very well see some red shiny guys.'

'But *you're* here, so I'm not afraid.'

'Exactly. It's a comforting tie I'm wearing, isn't it?'

'I like it very much.'

'And what do you think of my head?'

'Pardon?'

'Sorry. Not my head. My suit. That's what I meant to say. What do you think of my suit?'

'I wish I had one like it. Here I am in a whole new world called Nestor and I'm wearing pyjamas and slippers.'

A shadow falls over us. I look up to see the under-carriage of a wide floating vehicle. It moves slowly, barely fifty metres above us, and doesn't make a sound. Unhealthy-looking smoke billows from it.

'Public transport system,' Dr Vendra explains. 'First shuttle of the day, full of commuters. This place will be swarming in an hour.'

'How long is that?' I ask.

'How long is what?'

'An hour?'

The shuttle lands on top of the building.

'That is a remarkably odd question,' Dr Vendra says. 'An hour is an hour.'

'But if I spend, say, an hour here, does an hour pass on earth?'

'You'll see . . .'

'And why didn't you just teleport us straight to the building? Why do we have to walk so far?'

Dr Vendra shakes his head. I appear to be irritating him.

'Teleport? What does that mean? I'm not a magician, Colin. There's always some margin of error when using the infirmary, especially the inbound.'

Another of the shuttles floats smokily overhead. The yellow sky grows brighter. I can see more of the city now, as imperfect walls reflect light and cast shadows.

'The infirmary,' I say. 'Is that the space between my world and your world? Like the bridge between the universe and an alternative universe?'

'In a manner of speaking,' Dr Vendra says.

The building has unevenly spaced windows, many of which have been masked from the inside, as though the person forced to live with the window has decided they would prefer it did not admit light or offer a view. The giant metal doors that front the building don't quite meet. There is a gap between them, wide enough for a person to fit through. The doors are thick and constructed from solid metal. And yet there are pockmarks and dribbles where the doors have melted. It would take an incredible heat to do this.

Dr Vendra and I enter the building. The air is stale. There has been no attempt to make the foyer look glamorous or professional. Stuck to mildewed concrete walls are lists of the building's tenants. But they are unreadable. Half the names have been crossed out, or have ugly patches of rust obscuring the lettering.

'I'm on the ninth floor,' says Dr Vendra. 'If we're lucky they will have fixed the lift.'

My throat feels dry. 'Could I have water?'

'There's some in my office,' says Dr Vendra.

He opens a door, revealing a stairwell, and beckons.

'Aren't you going to try the lift?' I ask.

'I was joking,' says Dr Vendra. 'Those things haven't worked in centuries. We don't have electricity.'

I resign myself to climbing nine flights of stairs to get a cup of water.

The farther we climb, the more decrepit the stairwell becomes. The building is sick. Brown stains surround cracks in the walls. One of the steps crumbles as I plant my foot on it.

'Do people really work in this building?' I ask.

'Rigorously.'

'But it's so squalid.'

'It's the most beautiful building on our world. But yes, it's squalid.'

'Why are there no other people? Why haven't we seen anyone on the stair?'

'This is the up stairwell. The down stairwell is on the opposite side.'

'That doesn't really answer my question.'

'Citizens arrive by shuttle on the roof of the building. They descend the stairs to the level on which they work. Come the end of the working day, our stairwell will be teaming with workers ascending to the departure shuttles waiting above. Ah. Here we are.'

Dr Vendra pushes open a large door with a black number nine discernible on it. We walk through.

The corridors are uniformly grey, with a series of closed, smaller doors. The ceiling is low, and made of a type of pegboard that has mouldy growths.

'It's quiet,' I say.

'It's early,' Dr Vendra says. 'The shuttles have only just arrived. Citizens won't commence work for half an hour at least.'

We stop outside a door. Unlike the others, it is slightly ajar.

'It would seem my colleague has already arrived.' Dr Vendra twitches nervously. 'I hope I'm not in trouble for being unpunctual. My colleague can be . . . terse.' Dr Vendra collects himself and regards me with those powerful eyes. For the first time I realise they aren't any real colour, which is unusual for powerful eyes. 'Colin, I'm impressed by your composed reaction to what must seem a terribly alien world to you. Many people would find it disturbing.'

'I feel I know this place.'

'Interesting.'

'Is that possible?'

'No.'

'Maybe I saw it in a dream or something?'

'No.'

'Television show?'

'That would be too easy.'

'How do you mean?'

'Please, Colin, ask more important questions.'

'Could I please have a cup of water?'

'At once.'

But Dr Vendra hesitates and I become impatient. The thirst is so great.

'A warning, Colin,' he says at last.

'Dr Vendra?'

'Although you have been the picture of calm since we arrived, I fear that the next experience may alarm you. In the interests of maintaining a productive, dignified atmosphere, I would appreciate it if you could refrain from crying out or making any other sudden noises.'

Dr Vendra opens the door to reveal a stark office. The few items of furniture are drab. A piece of thick paper has been stuck over the window, so the yellow light from outside is filtered to an oppressive dimness. A red figure sits in the half-light. Though he is poorly illuminated, he shines. He rises to his hind legs, so that he stands the height of a man. He has long antennae and a carapace in which I fancy I see my reflection. Tiny hairs run along two pairs of forearms that end in claws. He is a cockroach.

'I'm Dr Maximew,' the cockroach says, in a voice that's deeper than Dr Vendra's, and thoroughly companionable.

'I'm Colin,' I say calmly.

'I do not frighten you?' says Dr Maximew.

'Not when I see you like this,' I say. 'And not when I hear you talk so nicely.'

'Excellent,' says Dr Vendra, behind me. 'Then I'm sure you won't mind if I dispense with my disguise. It is both painful and cumbersome.'

I am not surprised that Dr Vendra is also a giant, affable cockroach.

He passes me a cup of water. It tastes of carrot.

'Why did you want to see me?' I say, feeling exhausted yet relieved. Normally I hate cockroaches, but these aren't the predatory monsters that appear in my dreams and on the edges of my vision. I can tell they mean me no harm. And the fact that I see them vindicates me. They do exist. 'More importantly,' I say, 'why did you want me to see you?'

Dr Maximew and Dr Vendra smile. They don't even look that much like cockroaches. They resemble grasshoppers, except they're red. And everyone knows grasshoppers are friendly, with nice faces and big round eyes. Whoever heard of an evil grasshopper?

'Are you ready for an official tour of Nestor?' Dr Maximew asks.

CHAPTER 11

The war was over in five minutes. A world of forests and seas, gardens and lakes, human beings and animals was wiped out in less time than it took me to break into Dr Parkinson's office. I have been warned about the war. My hosts don't want me to be horrified when I see it for myself. It's coming.

For the moment I am enjoying a walk through the concourse in front of the building. The morning sun is bright, the sky a brilliant blue. I'm in a park with trees, birds and flowerbeds. The surrounding buildings are handsome and in good repair. Humans sit on benches, enjoying a quick lunch in the middle of their working day. I try to step out of the way when a determined boy on skates heads straight for me. He passes. Men and women who aren't in quite such a hurry sit under trees. Some of them have walkmans and nod to the music. Others lie in the grass and read. I can't make out the book covers. I'd like to know what they're reading. But the picture isn't crystal clear. Dr Vendra and Dr Maximew are showing me a scene from centuries ago. Sometimes the picture whites out altogether, like an old nitrate film that has decayed over the years.

One particular whiteout lasts for several seconds and I suspect that the 'official tour' might be over. Then the picture returns and I am flying over a city with sky-scrapers. Some are office buildings; others are blocks of apartments, with gardens on the rooftops. I even see a tennis court surrounded by large nets. It's on the top of an apartment block at least twenty storeys high. Another building has a rooftop pool. The streets are bustling with cars and people. It looks familiar. In the centre of the city is a vast reserve with a lake and fountains. It could almost be where I live.

After another whiteout I am back at the concourse, only this time the picture is not as clear. I am watching footage from a security camera. The picture is grey and uneventful. Then the blast comes. The buildings shake and some collapse altogether. People are crushed as walls of masonry rain down. There is no sound but I can imagine the screams as multitudes run away from the ugly clouds that were once solid buildings. The ground shakes and heaves upwards. People have nowhere to run. And this is only the beginning. This is the blast. What comes next is the heat: a searing white heat that melts metal and glass. Flesh and blood are fuel to heat like this. Everyone burns. Whiteout.

I'm seated between Dr Vendra and Dr Maximew. Each of them holds an antenna to my forehead. They have recreated these ancient images in my mind. Dr Maximew asks if I care to see more, but I've had enough. My chest hurts. Dr Vendra fetches me a cup of carroty water while Dr Maximew produces a cloth and wipes something from my forehead. It's a clear goo that the cockroaches must secrete. I try not to show my distaste, as I expect this would hurt the feelings of a highly evolved cockroach. Dr Maximew folds the cloth and places it on the desk.

'Some buildings remained standing,' Dr Maximew says. 'The one we currently occupy was built for humans in positions of great authority. It was made to last.'

I finish the cup of water.

'I read that the only life that would survive a nuclear war would be the cockroaches,' I say. 'I guess you guys have proved it. How did you get so big?'

Dr Vendra and Dr Maximew regard each other before answering.

'We evolved,' says Dr Maximew. 'But the radioactivity might have accelerated the process.'

I'm gripped by a cold panic. 'Radioactivity? Am *I* radioactive? Will I get sick?'

Dr Maximew is conciliatory. 'The war happened a long time ago. There is minimal radiation. You will be fine.'

I'm not convinced.

'Other humans have been here before you and we have seen no adverse effects,' Dr Vendra adds. He turns to Dr Maximew. 'Oh dear, should I have told him that?'

'There seems little point in retracting it now,' says Dr Maximew fussily.

'The radioactivity didn't affect them,' says Dr Vendra. 'Not in the short term, anyway.'

'And the long term?' I ask.

'We don't have the figures on that. Do we, Dr Maximew?'

'None at all, I'm afraid. But you needn't worry, Colin. You will not be staying long. Which brings us to why we brought you here. Please come to the window.'

I feel unsteady after being shown the harrowing images of war, but I stagger over to the square of yellow light. Dr Vendra removes the paper screen so that I have an uninterrupted view of the world outside. The concourse is now a seething mass of cockroaches. I shudder. These cockroaches do not look gentle and refined. They are rushing about, as if they are an infestation suddenly disturbed by the opening of a cupboard door. Then I realise that there *is* order in what they are doing. Some of the cockroaches are congregating as humans would. Pairs of cockroaches are deep in conversation. If they were humans they might be discussing sport. They have no electricity so they can't be talking about television. Maybe they're comparing notes on the rotting food they ate last night.

'How did it get so busy all of a sudden?' I ask.

'We have a rigid timetable,' says Dr Maximew. 'It is impossible to live without order. There are scheduled times for work, recreation –'

'Sexual intercourse,' adds Dr Vendra.

'Sleep,' adds Dr Maximew, sounding annoyed that Dr Vendra had said 'sexual intercourse'.

'Don't you just sleep when it gets dark?' I ask.

'It never gets dark. Just dimmer.'

'What about the humans you mentioned? Where are they?'

'We will come to that,' says Dr Vendra.

'You see a thousand of our kind down there,' says Dr Maximew, waving an elegant claw at the multitudes below. 'They seem model citizens. They work to the best of their ability, take no more than they need and share with others. But every society has its misfits. You realise this, I am sure.'

I nod. 'Do you have gangs with aerosols?'

'Aerosols?'

'Pressurised cans of paint. Kids use them to spray stuff on walls.'

'In that respect at least our culture is more advanced than yours,' says Dr Maximew. 'But we have recently learned of an underclass that has been disobeying our most basic law. This is *our* world. It may not seem attractive to you. Indeed, *we* may not seem attractive to you.'

'You look good for cockroaches,' I say. 'Better than I thought you would.'

Dr Vendra makes a clicking noise. He may even be flattered. He replaces the screen on the window. I admire the chitinous exoskeleton of his back. 'Chitinous' and 'exoskeleton.' Two more excellent words I have learned from books.

'We suffer privations here,' says Dr Maximew. 'But we accept this as our lot. The war destroyed most of this world. Even so it gave us the chance to evolve and form our own societies. This is where we belong.'

Dr Vendra offers me another cup of water and takes over the discourse.

'What's kept our respective worlds separate is an interstitial layer between the one and the other. It's called the infirmary.'

I drink some water and am surprised to find that it has a different taste from the carroty water in the first cup. It tastes like strawberry.

'Recently the infirmary was breached,' continues Dr Maximew. 'Until now, citizens knew nothing of your world, just as you knew nothing of ours. But a growing number of our citizens have become jealous. They don't see why they should live here when a more desirable world exists on the other side of the infirmary. Dr Vendra?'

'As you have experienced, Colin, the citizens of this world are not tangible in yours. When I put my hand on your shoulder, you didn't feel it because in your world my hand was not manifest. It was like a hologram.'

'It must be hard to be in a world where you can't touch anything,' I say.

'You don't know the half of it.' Dr Vendra shudders. It is intriguing to see a giant cockroach make a gesture so human.

'So if it's hard for you to exist in my world, why have I been seeing so many of you?' I ask.

'Strength in numbers,' says Dr Maximew.

'How many of them are on earth?'

'Hard to say. They cannot remain permanently and must return here, at least for the moment. They are always in minimum groups of one hundred.'

'And we humans walk right through them, never even realising?'

'Some of you are starting to notice,' says Dr Vendra. 'You in particular, Colin. Please don't be alarmed by what we're about to tell you.'

'You keep warning me. There's really no need. I'm from a psychiatric ward. I'm on medication. It takes a lot to alarm me.'

'I don't believe you should be on medication,' says Dr Maximew solemnly. 'It would be a good idea to stop taking it.'

'What is it you want to tell me? I promise I won't be alarmed.'

Dr Maximew paces, as though this helps him to deliver unpleasant news.

'Although they are hampered by a world where they lack corporeality,' he says, 'the energy generated by a large group is sometimes enough to –'

He pauses for dramatic effect, possibly a moment too long.

'Yes?' I prompt.

'– sometimes enough to move a human through the infirmary into *this* world.'

'They abduct people?'

'I'm afraid so.'

'Have I been abducted?'

Dr Vendra takes a step back. 'Of course not. You were invited and you came willingly. It's easy when people are compliant.'

It's true. Dr Vendra's sixth finger intrigued me. I wanted to see the third tail of the cat. I offered no resistance.

'The abducted humans are still on your world?' I ask.

'Yes.'

'Was Len abducted?'

'Len?'

'The whiny old bastard in Ward 44. He disappeared last night.'

'Whiny old bastard?' Dr Vendra enquires of Dr Maximew. 'Is there a whiny old bastard?'

'Too early to say,' Dr Maximew replies.

'What about Rodney Meaklin?' I say. 'That kid who disappeared in Anderston?' It had been on the news for a few weeks, till people grew tired of the story and moved on to fresher, more enticing tragedies.

'We don't know.'

'And what about Briony?'

Dr Maximew and Dr Vendra regard me with sad eyes.

'You loved her, didn't you?' says Dr Maximew.

I nod.

'Many humans have lost loved ones. I'm sorry, Colin. We do not know if she is here or not. The misfits brought many humans to Nestor, but we do not know where they are kept.'

'Are they safe?'

'We don't know that either.'

I'm angry. '*Why* don't you know? Aren't you brilliant scientists or something?'

'We toil hard,' says Dr Maximew, in a soothing tone. 'We will know soon.'

'Why are the humans being abducted in the first place?' I ask. My nose is running. My eyes start to water.

Dr Maximew looks out of the window, even though the screen has been replaced and the view obscured. He holds one pair of arms behind his back and taps his claws together.

'The recalcitrant citizens are working on a technology that will enable the physiology of a human to be bonded with their own. Once the process is complete, they will be able to enter *your* world and live there permanently. I cannot allow this to happen.'

'What do you want *me* to do?' I pick up Dr Maximew's cloth from the desk and wipe my nose with it.

Dr Maximew opens a drawer in the desk and takes out a small white case. He flips open the lid. The case contains two small pools of clear liquid.

'Have you ever worn contact lenses?' he asks.

'Never needed to.'

'You will grow accustomed to them.'

I take the case and see the tiny transparent disks immersed in the liquid.

'When you wear them, you'll have a clear view of the citizens who trespass in your world. They will be in full view. They will no longer hide in your peripheral vision. We trust this won't be too alarming, now that you have seen us up close.'

'But you're the *good* guys. I'll be seeing the bad guys.'

'Yes. Be brave.'

'I would prefer spectacles,' I say, looking nervously at the contact lenses and wondering what it will be like to stick my fingers into my eyes.

'Spectacles are too substantial to move from our world into yours,' says Dr Maximew.

'And when I see the shiny guys, what do I do?'

Dr Maximew stands alongside Dr Vendra and I notice the differences between them. Dr Maximew does not shine as brightly as Dr Vendra, and some of his hairs are grey. I wonder how long I will have to spend on Nestor before I can tell cockroaches apart at first glance.

'Well?' I remind them. 'What do I do when I see the bad guys?'

Dr Maximew gives an awkward twitch. 'We're not sure.'

'*That's* your plan?'

'We need *you* to work out how they can be destroyed. You come from a place with laws of physics that are beyond our grasp. We have only just learned about string theory, whereas to you it must seem obvious.'

'Not really,' I admit. 'I understand it about as well as quantum mechanics, or walking as an Olympic sport.'

'Then perhaps we will educate each other,' says Dr Maximew. 'The important thing is that we have made contact. You realise our intentions are good, just as we see goodness in you. We will work together to put an end to the outrage that is being inflicted upon your world and its people. Stay in the hospital until we contact you again. At present the recalcitrants seem to be amassing in the area you have just departed.'

'Ward 44?'

'You've noticed them yourself.'

'Why would they want to abduct mental patients?'

'The recalcitrants have methods that we do not fully understand. Perhaps these patients have something they seek? Perhaps they have unique talents that may be put to use here on Nestor?'

I shake my head. 'Not Len. He doesn't have any unique talents. Everyone on earth can fart.'

Dr Vendra makes a chuckling sound of which Dr Maximew clearly disapproves.

'These are questions you will help us to answer,' says Dr Maximew. 'Take care. If you require our assistance, find a portal to the infirmary. Dr Vendra will fetch you and bring you here.'

'How do I find a portal?'

'It will be a door that is unnaturally warm,' says Dr Maximew. 'Knock on it with anything made of metal and Dr Vendra will come. And do not speak of this to anyone, Colin. Your sister Briony may well be alive on Nestor, but keep it secret. Your parents cannot be told or it may jeopardise her safe return.'

'I give you my word,' I say.

'I'll escort you back,' says Dr Vendra.

I hesitate. 'Will I have to go down to the ground with all those cockroaches running about? No offence.

I think you are both extremely fine cockroaches, but I don't think I could move through a swarm of you.'

'You will have to get used to that, Colin, now that you have the lenses. One day the recalcitrants will appear before you. But it won't be necessary for you to go to the concourse. There is an outbound portal on this floor.'

Dr Vendra and I walk out of the office and into the corridor with the grey doors that seems to go on forever.

'A portion of the infirmary is laterally fixed here,' Dr Vendra says. 'Dr Maximew created it using your string theory. He is the wisest of all Nestorians.'

'I wondered what you guys called yourselves. Why didn't you tell me before?'

'I liked it when you referred to us as shiny guys. It has a nice ring.'

'So the portal is one of these doors?'

Dr Vendra nods.

'Which?'

'It keeps changing.'

Dr Vendra holds out a claw and taps on a door.

'Stone cold,' he says. 'There are ninety-nine more. It could take some time.'

CHAPTER 12

Dear Mr and Mrs Lapsley,

Thank you for your continued faith in our efforts here at Ward 44. Please rest assured that Colin is receiving the very best treatment possible.

A pharmacological approach to Colin's depression has yielded gradual, positive results. However, after a period of four weeks, we would hope to see greater improvement in the patient, hence the change in our methodology, as discussed. My feeling is that Colin's innate depression may have become aggravated by other, more complex psychological factors. But I am confident that we are taking the correct approach and that Colin will make good progress. Many of our patients have found the treatment beneficial, and I am happy to answer any questions you may have.

Once again, I offer my deepest sympathies. My staff and I are aware of how difficult it must be for you, especially in light of recent events. This has been a tragic time, and our hearts go out to you. Please feel free to visit whenever it suits you.

Yours sincerely,

Dr Joshua L Parkinson

CHAPTER 13

I wake up in bed, unaware of the time.

It's hard to open my eyes. I almost have to lift up my eyelids by hand. My sight is slightly blurred. Then I remember the contact lenses that I now wear. I must prepare myself to see giant cockroaches in front of me, not just out of the corner of my eye. It comes back to me – how I returned to Ward 44 from Nestor. I walked through the correct doorway on the ninth floor, and emerged seconds later from the cabinet beside my bed. I had to crouch to get through it. I remember now. It's wondrous to think that two doors from such different dimensions could be no more than thirty centimetres apart.

I splash my eyes with water from the cup on my cabinet, and wipe it away with the sheet. I can see clearly. The bed opposite is empty, but Len's half-finished basket is still there. Since the beds in Ward 44 are so precious, I'm surprised that the bed hasn't been filled.

Shamita, the Indian nurse, looks in and tells me I must put on clean pyjamas and take my old ones to the laundry. I have been wearing these ones for too long. It's important for me to take pride in my appearance, she adds. It will help me get well. It's one of Dr Parkinson's rules.

Patients are allocated two pairs of pyjamas. We are not allowed to have any more. Having just two pairs of pyjamas teaches us order and routine. We wake up; we change out of our old pyjamas into the clean ones that we keep in our bedside cabinet. When we've changed into the clean pyjamas, we take the old ones to the laundry. At the end of the day we collect the cleaned pyjamas and put them back into the bedside cabinet. The process is repeated every morning. That's how it's supposed to work, but some patients are slack. They wear the same pyjamas for two or three days, which troubles the nurses, especially Shamita. Patients that can't supply their own underclothes are given hospital ones. Mango calls them his psycho-undies.

I change my pyjamas under the blanket on my bed, since I don't want to subject anyone to my pale naked body, least of all myself. No one knows this, but I've stolen a *third* pair of clean pyjamas. I took them from a pallet of brand-new pyjamas that had been delivered. They are my insurance, in case I piss myself. It happens from time to time. Not regularly, but it does happen.

I walk down the corridor, carrying my pyjamas in a bundle. I look into various bedrooms. Jill is still asleep. I feel sorry for her. She keeps running herself down, saying she's no good at anything. She feels ugly and uncoordinated and useless.   .

Mango once did something kind for Jill. He got her to play a game of pool with him. Jill said she was unable to play, that she was too stupid, but Mango told her anyone could play. He taught her simple things, such as how to chalk a cue and hold it correctly. Mango is a good pool player. When he played with Jill he was very encouraging. He gave her multiple free shots, saying these were the rules. He deliberately fudged easy shots, refusing to sink a ball until Jill had sunk one. And when the eight ball was left on the table, Mango pretended to hit it badly, until Jill sank the ball herself. Mango said she was a star. Val flattered her as well. Jill smiled for the first time since she had been admitted. Then Len spoiled everything by telling Jill that Mango let her win. He had played deliberately badly. Jill's happiness melted, and she looked at Mango as though he had betrayed her. Maybe it was wrong of Mango to play badly. Jill would learn sooner or later that she had been allowed to win. A doctor may not have approved of what Mango had done, but I did.

The laundry is downstairs, in a part of the building where nurses like Keith go to smoke. They aren't allowed to smoke inside the building. But down here in the basement is an exit door with a keycard lock. I've seen Keith here, propping the door open and puffing away.

The basement is perfectly square, like a cut-off footprint of the ward. The wall that marks its internal boundary also has a door, though it's permanently locked and I've never seen anyone use it. Whatever is behind that door is a mystery. Perhaps the door isn't *meant* to be opened? The basement ceiling is low, as though the space were designed to be a carpark. But no one parks here. There is a wide roller door where the trucks come to make deliveries. I've watched from the shadows, hoping to steal something.

I dump my dirty pyjamas in the skip outside the laundry. There's a sign on the door. It says INFIRMARY LAUNDRY. I'm surprised. I'd forgotten that I'd seen the word 'infirmary' before. Dr Vendra and Dr Maximew used the word so well when they described the interstitial layer between our worlds. 'Infirmary' is the perfect name for it, because the layer is intangible and unstable, a force that exists but cannot be held or felt. It doesn't seem right to see such a good word on an old laundry door. Has the word been there all the time, or am I being sent a message from Nestor? If the door is hot, it could be an entrance to the infirmary between worlds. I touch the door briefly with a fingertip. Then I push it open. The washers and driers are huge, powerful machines. The nurses use them to launder their own clothes from home, not just their uniforms. Tim tells me that nurses don't get paid well. He thinks he should take whatever perks he can, and if that means saving coin laundrette money by using the machines at work, what's the problem with that? Thinking of Tim and admiring his attitude, I leave the laundry.

The air down here is still and smells stale. It reminds

me of the air on Nestor. This would be the perfect place for the shiny guys to gather. I'm wearing the contact lenses. I'll be able to see them if they're here. But I'm alone.

On the grimy concrete stairs there's a handrail for the elderly and infirm. Some hospitals have been sued lately for negligence. Not long after I arrived, I thought about throwing myself down these stairs. I didn't want to kill myself. Not exactly. I just wanted to damage myself so that my parents could sue the hospital. They're not poor, but the money would be of more use to them than I am.

Today I don't have such dark thoughts, because I understand things better. I know what *really* happened to Briony. She was abducted by giant cockroaches and taken to another world. Dr Vendra and Dr Maximew explained it all to me. If Briony is alive on Nestor, I can bring her back.

The excitement makes my hands shake. I think of what a family reunion would be like, with so much to talk about. Briony would have amazing tales about what it was like to spend three years on an alternative world, while we believed she was dead. Not only have Dr Vendra and Dr Maximew given me hope, they've given me a mission. I alone must find the Nestorians that trespass in our world and kidnap people. Once I find them, I will think of a way to stop them. Abductions will cease. I will be a hero.

In the meantime, I will obey Dr Maximew and tell no one, except Mango. He and I made a vow: we will tell each other everything. There will be no secrets between us. Mango told me about the youth training centre where he started a riot before he was sent to Ward 44. I told him about my pathetic suicide attempt. He made me swear that I will never try anything like that again.

I don't know what time it is. I walk down the corridor in the direction of the dining room. Alcoholic Val approaches, in grey pyjamas that look tight. My own pyjamas are ridiculously baggy and if I didn't keep retying my pants, they would fall down. This happened once in the recreation room, while I was playing pool with Mango. I leaned over to use the cue rest and my pyjama pants fell down to reveal my undershorts. Everyone killed themselves laughing. I'd done it deliberately, of course. I *wanted* to make people laugh. But they didn't know that. I hate showing my body but the opportunity had been too good to pass up. People still talk about it.

I ask Val what time it is and she tells me lunch has just finished. If I hurry, there might still be some for me. Val compliments me on my hair. It's quite long now. She says it makes me look a bit like Jesus but I shouldn't go getting ideas.

Half the patients are in the dining room. Anthea is absent. Mango is sitting alone as usual, because people don't want him to hug them. My tray is not there. I realise that Mango has taken it, fearing the food might go to waste in my absence. I sit alongside him.

'Hello, spazzo.'

'Hello, mental case.'

Mango pushes my tray towards me and we share

the plate of steamed vegetables and dumplings in gravy. I have so much to tell him. My mouth is dry and I find it hard to swallow.

There's no one in the courtyard.

'Let's go outside,' I say. 'I've got important news.'

I look around. There aren't any Nestorians about. But I know it's just a matter of time. They will appear and I will be ready . . .

CHAPTER 14

Q. Anthea, you look well today. Have you eaten?

A. Yes.

Q. What did you have for breakfast?

A. Cornflakes.

Q. How do you feel?

A. About the cornflakes?

Q. Do you feel better than when we last spoke?

A. I guess so.

Q. Have you seen any shadows that aren't there?

A. Not so many. Not up close.

Q. Why do you think the shadows have kept their distance?

A. Because of the pills you give me.

Q. You seem concerned about that.

A. If I stop taking the pills, won't the shadows come back worse than ever? Like with the speed?

Q. These pills are different.

A. This is a psychiatric ward.

Q. Yes, it is.

A. Dr Quayle, why am I in a psychiatric ward? I took an accidental overdose. People are always doing that. Why am I here?

Q. . . . I think your father was rather keen –

A. That makes sense.

Q. – not to mention worried –

A. This place is really boring.

Q. I'm glad you think so.

A. Glad?

Q. It's a positive sign. What would you like to do? We have a library, a gym, arts and crafts – what do you like?

A. Netball.

Q. That may be difficult.

A. I know. Everyone here's mental.

Q. But you could practise. There's a basketball hoop in the gym.

A. How often do I have to see you?

Q. Every morning. You will receive a weekly timetable. All mealtimes are listed.

A. Great.

Q. I'd like you to eat.

A. You sound like my parents.

Q. That's because I want you to be well. I'd also like you to keep busy.

A. Weaving baskets?

Q. I'm sorry about that. We had a proper art room but there was asbestos. So it's basket-weaving as an interim measure. Of course, there are other activities –

A. I hate these pyjamas.

Q. Dr Parkinson believes –

A. Dr Parkinson sounds like a control freak.

Q. The pyjamas don't look so bad on you.

A. Would you wear them?

Q. Maybe around the house.

A. Shopping?

Q. No.

A. Where do you normally shop?

Q. The mall.

A. You'd fit right in.

CHAPTER 15

Mango and I sit at the courtyard table. I swear Mango to secrecy before I tell him everything that has happened. I explain about Dr Vendra and Dr Maximew and the barren world where the Nestorians live. The Nestorians, I clarify, are the shiny guys I've been seeing. I take particular care in describing the post-apocalyptic landscape of Nestor, the infirmary that separates one world from the other, and doors that are only thirty centimetres apart in different dimensions. I explain to Mango that I'm wearing contact lenses that were supplied by the Nestorians. (Mango is impressed when I tell him that the Nestorians look like giant cockroaches. I thought he'd like that part.) The lenses allow me to see the Nestorians that have infiltrated *this* world.

I ask Mango if my eyes seem different and he tells me they look a bit diluted. He means dilated, but I don't correct him. Mango isn't great with words, but he has other talents. He can drive a car. I don't know how to do that, only how to start one without a key.

Mango wants to know if I can see the cockroach guys now. I look around. I see Tim pushing the medication trolley. He smiles at me. I see Anthea walking into the dining room to get water. She doesn't smile at anyone. She's still too new. When she does start to smile, it will probably be at Mango, because he's okay looking. Even when he hasn't brushed his hair, it looks good because it's straight and sticks up. Mango can't take his eyes off Anthea. I know there's no point in continuing the conversation until she's left the dining room, which she does without looking our way.

'I don't see any cockroach guys at the moment,' I tell Mango. 'We should probably start calling them Nestorians. And here's the amazing part. The bad Nestorians are taking people from our world into theirs.'

I have Mango's undivided attention. 'You mean they're abducting people?'

'Yes. They abducted Briony. They probably took Rodney Meaklin as well. And Len. They're taking humans to Nestor because they want to take something from their bodies and put it into their own. It's so the Nestorians can survive in *this* world.'

When I put it like this, I actually scare myself. The image is too horrible.

'Did you see the abducted humans?' asks Mango. 'When you were in the cockroach place?'

'No. But Dr Maximew and Dr Vendra told me they are hidden. They're looking for them.'

'What are you supposed to do if you see one of the

cockroach guys in *this* world?'

'Nestorians,' I say.

'Yeah.'

'Dr Vendra and Dr Maximew haven't worked it out. They want *me* to.'

'You're good at working stuff out.'

Mango understands about abductions because he was abducted himself when he was a kid. There's a whole week of his life that he doesn't remember. He thinks it must have been aliens, and hopes he wasn't probed.

'So how come they abducted you, then let you come back?' asks Mango.

'They didn't abduct me. I went voluntarily. These two Nestorian doctors are on *our* side.'

'Right.' Mango looks reflective. 'You really think Len was abducted?'

'It makes sense. That's why I was seeing so many Nestorians around the hospital. They have to work together. It takes a hundred of them to abduct a single human. You believe me, don't you?'

'I will always believe you,' says Mango. 'I believe you when you say you will help me find the impossible cupboard. I know that will happen one day.'

'It will.'

'Your eyes are watering.'

I wipe them. 'It's just the lenses. I'm not used to wearing them.'

I feel a chest pain and press my hand hard on my thorax.

'Are you okay?' Mango asks.

'My chest feels funny.'

I notice there are fruitcake crumbs on Mango's pyjamas.

'How long have I been gone?' I ask.

'About an hour.'

It's impossible. I think of what I've seen and experienced.

'I was here an hour ago?' I say.

'Sure. You went off with Tim.'

Time on Nestor must pass slowly, compared with time in our dimension. I look at my slippers, checking for dust from the other world. There is none. The only proof of my visit is the contacts I wear. I don't even know if I can take them out. Someone yells.

'You are in a shitload of trouble.'

It's Len, leering as he struts into the courtyard.

'They must have brought him back,' says Mango, with genuine sadness.

There's a white pocket calculator on Dr Parkinson's desk. He picks it up and types:

$$55378008$$

Then he turns the calculator upside-down to reveal the word he has magically created in the liquid crystal window:

$$8008LE55$$

Every kid with a calculator knows this gag, but I laugh, because I presume this is what Dr Parkinson wants, even though I'm in a shitload of trouble.

'That is what we call a joke,' says Dr Parkinson. 'It's

funny. I know you like jokes and how important they are to you, so it's vital that you learn the difference between what is funny and what isn't.'

'Okay.'

'It *wasn't* funny that you had everyone thinking Len had vanished. You upset a lot of people.'

Dr Parkinson looks like a petulant boy.

'I told the truth about Len,' I say. 'And I gave you the clue about the basket. I told you that he wouldn't have left the building without it.'

'You knew where he was the whole time.'

'I didn't. I really didn't.'

'Colin, Len has explained it. You exploited him. You gave him the stolen keycard. You told him to use it to get to the other building. No one looked for him there because no one knew a keycard had been taken. He said you gave him a chocolate bar to do it. He didn't have the clarity to realise what he was doing was wrong.'

'That isn't what happened.'

Dr Parkinson is about to sigh again but checks himself. 'All right, Colin. *You* tell me what happened.'

'Well, I did steal the keycard.'

'Yes.'

'Someone left it lying around at the nurses' station.'

Dr Parkinson raises an eyebrow. The disbelieving look is one he can pull off quite well.

'Okay, it wasn't lying around. I crept in and unlocked one of the drawers with a paperclip.'

'What else have you stolen?'

'Nothing.'

'We have your clothes, Mango's clothes and the magazines and books from under your bed. And the jam. Why did you steal packets of jam?'

'I don't know.' (But of course I do know. I was going to use the jam as fake blood in a prank. I just hadn't worked out the prank yet.)

'Don't you think it's selfish to deprive the other patients of jam?'

I nod in shame.

'Your clothes and Malcolm's clothes are back in the property cupboard, which has a new lock. This is all very discouraging.'

'I'm sorry. I did take some stuff, but I've been set up.'

'Colin, I like you and I certainly don't wish to transfer you. But I will *not* allow you to disrupt the valuable work we are doing here. *Do not* steal. *Do not* roam the ward at night. If you can't sleep, go to the nurses' station and someone will assist you. *Do not* give ideas to impressionable patients like Len.'

'I didn't give the keycard to Len. He stole it from my hiding place. I'm sorry that everyone is upset, but that's what Len wants. He hates me. It was *his* idea to stage his own disappearance. I didn't have anything to do with it.'

Dr Parkinson turns away. 'This has been most embarrassing for me.'

I understand now. After the business of the angry patient assaulting Keith, and now the theft of the keycard, Dr Parkinson has been reprimanded. Ward 44, his bold experiment, is not such a perfect place after all. No wonder he's angry with me. But Dr Parkinson is also clever. He knows that I'm onto him. He tries to hide his anger.

'When I grew up we didn't bother locking our doors,' he says.

I nearly fall out of my chair. 'Where on earth did you grow up?'

'A small town called Darnum in West Gippsland.'

'I've not heard of it.'

'It was a very nice place. Not many people there, but we all knew each other and helped each other out. A bit like here. I like to think so, anyway. It's how I see Ward 44 operating. I have very fond memories of my youth.'

'And yet you moved away.'

'Well, I wanted to be a psychiatrist. Darnum was a little dairy town.'

'I guess there wouldn't be much call for cow psychiatrists?'

Dr Parkinson picks up the paperclip and gazes at it. 'No, I'd say that most of the cows were well-adjusted.'

'They were happy just being cows. They didn't want to be ducks or –'

'Cows. That's what they wanted to be.'

'Where did you move? When you left Darnum?'

'Carlton. Where I went to university.'

'And did you lock your doors in Carlton?'

'I didn't have stuff that was worth stealing.'

'Did people steal it anyway?'

'Constantly. I could never understand. People stole things that were worthless. Someone stole a broken TV.'

'They probably didn't know it was broken.'

'The screen was smashed. No right-thinking human being would believe it was functional. It had fallen over at a party and I hadn't worked out what to do with it. So I left it sitting there. None of us watched television anyway. Then someone broke in and took it. What's the point of that, Colin?'

'I don't know, Dr Parkinson.'

'Will you promise me you won't steal again?'

'You have my word.'

'Is there anything else you want to tell me? Or ask me?'

'No, there's nothing else,' I say.

'We're all in it together,' he says.

But his catchphrase lacks conviction.

My mind races as I leave Dr Parkinson's office. For the first time I feel elated after seeing him, even though I have just been disciplined. My life has changed so much in the last few hours. There is a vicious alien scheme that only I can prevent, and there is also the wonderful possibility that I might see Briony again, and that I may even be her saviour. Minor distractions such as stealing Dr Parkinson's texta are no longer of any importance. Nevertheless, I do have it up my sleeve. I took it while he was typing that number into his pocket calculator.

CHAPTER 16

I like working in the library. Three times a week I help 99, the librarian, to make sure that the books are shelved according to the Dewey Decimal Classification System. 99 isn't the librarian's real name, but I call her that because she has hair like Barbara Feldon in *Get Smart*. If 99 were a book she'd be one 'notable for its format'.

99 loves her books. She's upset when one of them is returned with a torn page or food stains. Together we repair the damaged books as best we can and return them to their correct place on the numbered shelves. 100 is for philosophy. 200 is for religion. 300 is for social sciences. There are very few books on these shelves. But when we get up to 500, which is science, the shelves look healthier. My favourite shelves are the 800s, the ones for literature. There are so many 800 books that they occupy two whole shelves of their own. I can tell these are 99's favourites too, because she gets especially upset when an 800 book is damaged. She has so little

money to buy books, she complains. Why don't people take care of the ones she has? Because I hate to see 99 upset, I look after the books that I borrow.

99 can't believe that I have been so careless as to put a book about Princess Diana on the 200s shelf. Since when was Princess Diana a religion? I shelve it correctly. I am distracted because Anthea is in the library, reading an Anne Rice book. It's called *The Vampire Lestat* and it has only just come out.

Anthea and I haven't met properly. The first time she was freaked out and the second time she was asleep, so that doesn't count. She looks at peace, reading about vampires who have scruples and are drop dead gorgeous.

I sit at the table where Anthea sits, but not too close. I know not to invade someone's personal space. Vampires may well behave that way, but I don't. On my way to the table I've collected a book called *Large Rigs*. I should have paid more attention to my choice. When I open it, I see that it is clearly intended for slow readers. There are photos of trucks and captions that inform us of vital matters, such as the fact that trucks frequently travel on roads. If I pretend to be interested in this book, Anthea will think I'm slow. I should've brought the book about Princess Diana because she's so popular and eternal and we could have started a conversation about her. 'Did you know that trucks travel on roads?' is a rotten way to start a conversation. Apologising is better.

'I'm sorry,' I say.

Anthea looks up from her book.

'Sorry?' she says.

'I freaked you out when you arrived.'

'I don't remember much about that.'

'I'm Colin,' I say.

'I do remember that.'

'You're Anthea.'

'Last time I looked,' she says, looking as though she's about to go back to reading.

'I notice you like vampires,' I say.

'Yes.' She indicates my book. 'Do you like trucks?'

'Not passionately. Though it's interesting to know that trucks travel on roads.'

I show Anthea the page with the caption and photo of a truck. She knows I'm making a joke. She smiles. It's a nice smile.

'Why would someone put that in a book?' she says.

'Well, I guess there are some people who don't realise. They might think that trucks travel on clouds or marmalade.'

Anthea chuckles.

'This part of the book tells us that trucks often carry things. This is also reassuring. Trucks are enormous and slow. Car drivers hate to get stuck behind them. But since the truck is carrying something, like refrigerators, drivers accept that the truck is simply doing its job. People need refrigerators.'

Anthea hasn't told me to go away yet, which is encouraging.

'It must be very difficult for vampires to drive trucks,' I say. 'They would only be able to do it at night. Before the sun rises the vampires would have to bury themselves. Then what would happen to the truck? It might be stolen. When the vampire truckie comes to life again at night, his entire consignment of refrigerators could be hundreds of kilometres away. This is why there are no vampire truckies.'

'You're an idiot,' says Anthea, in the nice way that Briony used to say it.

'Thank you. Do you like it here?'

'You have a strange way of speaking. Where are you from? Are you English?'

'I come from a mystical place called Frankston.'

Anthea laughs out loud and 99 wants to know what the fuss is about. I explain that Anthea and I were discussing Frankston, and ask if there are any books on the subject. They would, of course, be located on the 900 shelf.

'Sorry, we don't have anything on Frankston,' says 99. 'I've spent my budget for the year. I could buy a book about Frankston in the next financial year, but that's five months away and you may not be here.'

99 returns to her desk.

I try a bold move. 'Anthea, do you think vampires are real?'

'Only in books and movies.'

'So you don't see vampires out of the corner of your eyes?'

'That's a strange question. I don't see vampires.'

'But you do see something. Don't you?'

The conversation stalls. Anthea goes over to the desk to check out the vampire book. I join her, even though I have nothing to check out. I still have Franz Kafka's *The*

Castle and I am yet to reach the last sentence.

'Sorry, I shouldn't have asked that,' I say. 'Too personal. Can you play pool?'

'No,' says Anthea.

'My friend Mango is an extremely good pool player. He's the big guy with the sandy hair.'

Anthea nods. 'I've seen you together.'

'You should get Mango to teach you. He taught me and he is a brilliant teacher.'

99 checks out Anthea's book and asks her nicely to take care of it, because it's popular and there will be other patients who'll want to read it. Anthea promises to respect the book.

'Do you want to borrow that, Colin?' asks 99, a puzzled expression on her face.

I am still carrying *Large Rigs*.

I shake my head. 'There's no point. Someone told me the ending.'

I look out for Nestorians in the courtyard, but they are yet to appear. Mango has taken off his pyjama top so that he can enjoy the sunlight. I catch Tim looking at Mango from time to time, especially when he takes off his top in the courtyard. Tim is nice and gentle to everyone so I figure he's probably gay. Anthea approaches. Mango is startled when, out of the blue, Anthea asks if he could teach her how to play pool.

'He can also teach weight-lifting,' I say.

Anthea says she would prefer to play pool.

*

An hour later, Mango and I are in the gym, with some of the older guys. Keith is supervising. Mango is serious about bodybuilding and I'm not. He bench presses four times the weight that I do. He has decided to be my personal trainer, and makes me do some of the exercises with him. I keep telling him that I don't care if my body doesn't get bigger, that I don't see the point of lifting weights. Mango explains that I'm more likely to get a girlfriend if I'm not scrawny. But I don't want a girlfriend. I don't want anyone. It would only turn out bad. When I was a kid I was crazy about C3PO, the golden robot from the *Star Wars* movies. I wanted a friend like him, someone who was funny and trustworthy. But even a relationship with a robot would probably end badly for me. It would start seeing other robots behind my back, or whore around with vacuum cleaners.

When I don't pay close attention to Mango as he instructs me, he gets annoyed and sometimes Keith comes over because he's concerned there might be a quarrel. It's the only time Mango loses it with me, when I don't copy his correct way of doing dumbbell concentration curls or tricep bench dips.

At the end of the weight-lifting, Mango and I do sit-ups and throw a medicine ball to each other. When I lie back, I look at the ceiling, where the roman rings hang down. There is a mysterious hook attached to the ceiling, not far from the rings. I don't know what it's for, but I'll figure it out.

After fifty sit-ups, Mango brings the session to an end. He will be teaching Anthea how to play pool in the recreation room at five o'clock. He's excited, and grateful that I helped to set it up for him. But I tell him he needs to wear better pyjamas. The ones he's wearing have milk and food stains. He might make a bad impression. He should put on his other pair. Mango looks downcast. He has not washed his other pair. The ones in his cabinet are as bad as the ones he's wearing. I think about this; then tell Mango I'm about to do him an immense favour.

I'm prepared to sacrifice my *very best* pyjamas for him, not just freshly laundered ones. I will bring him the pristine pair that I hid under one of the couch cushions in the recreation room. When I get to the recreation room, I see Anthea toying nervously with the four-ball. She's waiting for Mango. She smiles, and I smile back. Somehow I have to distract her so she doesn't realise I'm retrieving a pair of stolen pyjamas. I have to lift up the cushion of a couch and take out a pair of contraband pyjamas without her knowing. As usual, a coin is the answer.

I walk over to Anthea and promise to show her something interesting. I take the coin out of my slipper and do a classic palm switch and an underside walk. It's really simple stuff, but she's so impressed. (I'll save the shuttle pass for later because that takes some preparation.) She actually claps, so I do a modest bow and then go to put the coin in my slipper. I deliberately drop it. My timing couldn't be better. The coin rolls under the couch, exactly as I planned. I pretend that I'm embarrassed and ask Anthea if she can help me get the coin back. I'll tilt the couch so that Anthea can grab the coin.

She gets down on her hands and knees and I tilt the couch, which is hard work for a weak guy like me. Anthea reaches for the coin. Holding the couch with my left hand, I slip the perfectly pressed pyjamas out from under the cushion with my right. Then I toss them over Anthea's head and out the door. I cough to cover the minimal sound of the pyjama package landing in the corridor. (You'd be surprised how many magic tricks are as basic as this.) The whole thing takes no more than a couple of seconds. Anthea stands and I put down the couch. She holds out the coin and I notice there is lint on her. The floor under the couch must be dirty. Guiltily, I tell her that she can keep the coin. I have others. I'd like to brush some of the lint off her, but I need to get away quickly so I can pick up the pyjamas in the corridor before anyone else does.

When I get back to the gym, Mango has finished his shower. He is checking himself out in the mirror. He isn't wearing a towel or anything. He really likes the way he looks and doesn't mind if other guys know it.

'I got you the very best pair of pyjamas in the entire universe,' I say.

Mango wants to be naked for a bit longer. He doesn't like his abdominals. With hands calloused from bodybuilding, he bundles up the fat around his navel, looks down at it and curses. He complains that he had a six-pack before he came to Ward 44, but they serve such crappy food that he is losing definition. (I don't suggest that if he didn't eat double servings of the crappy food he'd probably still have his six-pack.) It's not a major imperfection. Apart from the podgy tummy, Mango likes what he sees.

I wonder what it must be like to enjoy your reflection. Sometimes I go for days without looking in a mirror. I'd probably have trouble picking me in a police line-up. I haven't even told *you* what my face is like, or what colour my eyes are. You're halfway through this story and you don't even know what colour my hair is. Are my ears pointy? Have I a weak chin? Are there pimples on my forehead? You don't know.

Mango climbs into the pyjamas. The creases are sharp. There is no pilling because they are yet to be laundered. He looks good. No, he looks *fantastic*. At last he realises what an immense favour I've done for him. Mango thanks me profusely and goes off to teach Anthea how to be a pool shark. I wait for Keith to leave before I take Mango's old pyjamas out of the shower block.

I try to figure out where to hide the pyjamas because I don't want to go all the way to the laundry. I decide to stow them under the vaulting horse, in the same way the POWs hid their stuff in *The Great Escape*. I'll retrieve the pyjamas tomorrow and take them to the laundry; that is, if I am not busy fighting the recalcitrant aliens.

That night, I feel uplifted by the new focus in my life. When we are all gathered in the dining room, I tell everyone that before we eat I would like to say grace. Patients look surprised. Val thinks this is a lovely idea. I close my eyes, clasp my hands and recite with quiet dignity:

'While shepherds watched their flocks by night
All seated on the grass,
The angel of the Lord came down
And kicked them up the arse. Amen.'

Mango and Anthea burst out laughing. Even apologetic Jill cracks a smile. Val and Len, who sit together, are clearly not amused. Val tells me that there will be a day of judgment, and I won't be let into heaven. This is fine by me. The place is probably full of reformed alcoholics.

My stolen magazines haven't been confiscated. I guess they're too out of date for the nurses, but not too out of date for the waiting room. I idly flip through one as I lie in bed. A picture in one of the magazines takes me by surprise. It's Dr Vendra, in his human disguise, advertising vodka. I realise I've seen this ad before, on billboards and buses. I wonder why I didn't realise till now. It's probably because my mind is becoming clearer. Tonight I only pretended to take my medication, as advised by Dr Vendra and Dr Maximew.

For the first time in my life I miss the sound of Len snoring. This is because he is making other, less pleasant noises in the bed opposite.

'You'll never pull my big toe again, you little bastard, will you?' Len taunts from the other side of the room.

I wish the recalcitrants had abducted Len. But I know they're planning something.

CHAPTER 17

Dear Simon,

It wasn't speed. It was ketamine. Trevor said it was horse tranquilliser and it was the most amazing party drug ever. How did people discover this? Did a vet decide that if a drug could make a horse unconscious it might be fun to stick up your nose? Trevor said ketamine was way better than speed, and he was an expert.

Natasha's parents were away for the weekend. By the time we got to the party, three guys were already skinny-dipping in the pool. They kept calling out to the girls, asking them to join in. What is it with guys? They think nudity is a kind of virus. If they take off their clothes, it's just a matter of time before the girls catch the virus and they strip off too. That seems to be the theory. I haven't seen it work, but they never give up trying.

Inside the house the air was hot and sticky, and music throbbed. One of the toilets was out of action because a guy had passed out on the seat and no one could move him. People ran up to Trevor when the word got around that he'd arrived. Natasha eagerly held out her money. She smiled at me as if we were friends but I think she invited me to her party because I was with Trevor. I don't know how many bags of speed he sold, but there was no shortage of customers. He told me this was a good night, and that he wished he'd brought more stuff to sell. But he wasn't selling the ketamine. That was for us alone.

A lot of my friends thought it was weird to have such an old boyfriend. Trevor was in his twenties, six years older than me. He was good-looking; no one could deny that. We'd been together four months. I think I stuck with him because my dad hated him so much. Trevor wasn't even my type. He never read a book. He never went to a movie. But he was a good dancer. I like guys who can dance. And when we took speed on the weekend, the shadows that bothered me would disappear. On Tuesday, however, they came back.

There were now five guys in the pool, calling out desperately for some girls to join them. The guys would have been my age but they seemed much younger. Maybe being with Trevor had matured me. I recognised two of them from school. They looked better in blazers.

Trevor and I seemed to be the only people at the party who hadn't taken anything. He led me to a dark corner of the garden. The ketamine would be our secret. He warned me how strong it was. Imagine the head of a pin, he said, and the tiny amount of powder it could hold. That was all that was needed. He had a special little bottle designed to restrict the dose. It was called a bumper.

Trevor went first. He shook the bumper, sniffed hard, and then passed it to me. He rubbed his hands over his cheekbones. It meant he was high already. But it didn't work for me. I shook the bumper and took two more sniffs. Still nothing. Trevor was dazed and smiling, and I could see he wanted to dance. I gave him the bumper. We should go inside, I said, to see if we can persuade someone to let us have a line of speed.

As we walked back to the house, I sniffed and felt a strong chemical taste running down the back of my throat. Trevor said that was the taste of ketamine. I was about to have an incredible experience. I'd taken triple the dose he'd recommended. But they were such tiny amounts. How could there be a problem?

We were dancing when it happened. The party became like a movie. Every now and then the image would skip, as though part of the movie had been edited out. I felt incredible. Everything around me seemed to move farther and farther away. The movie soundtrack inside my head began to distort. Trevor was speaking, but his voice came out in growls. He was angry. Then fearful. How much had I taken? How much?

I'm told it was Trevor who drove me to casualty. He left me on the footpath and just drove off. He should have stayed, even if only for a short while, to make sure I was okay. But he fled. I *really* hope my dad doesn't find him. I don't think he will. Trevor is good at disappearing. That suits me fine. I don't want to see him again.

So here I am in Ward 44. I shoot a hundred baskets every day. I eat breakfast. I take medication. I do occupational therapy. My bad shadows are still there, but they're not as bad as they used to be.

There are two single beds in my room. In the bed opposite is an old lady called Val and she has all these pictures of Jesus around her bed, including a three-dimensional one with a floating heart. Actually, Jesus looks a bit like Trevor in this picture. It's weird when Our Lord and Saviour looks like your ex-boyfriend who dumped you outside the hospital. I asked Val if she was deeply religious. She said yes, and added that I was beautiful enough to be a runway model. I told Val I wanted to be a cat doctor and asked her what *she* did for a living. Val told me she was an alcoholic.

Most of the people here are old and mental, like Val. But there's a big guy called Mango who's seventeen. He's teaching me to play pool. The nurses told me that Mango has a problem where he grabs hold of people and hugs them but I shouldn't worry. He's a nice guy, though sometimes he looks at me the way Trevor used to, when we first started seeing each other. That's okay. I can deal with it if he starts to get serious.

There is another boy called Colin. I can't work him out. He's about my age. He annoyed me at first. He talks too much and he has a fake accent. He pouts. His hair is cut in a fringe, but it suits him. I like his smile. I wonder what sort of clothes he'd wear if he didn't have to dress in grey pyjamas. He's slender. Tee-shirts wouldn't suit him. He'd look good in a loose green shirt with a collar and long sleeves. I doubt that he wears bright colours, but maybe he should. He does magic tricks. He really comes alive when he does magic tricks.

I know Mum is upset and Dad is angry. I feel bad about that, but not shadow-bad. Please let them know I'm okay.

xxA

CHAPTER 18

Mrs Polidori, our basket-weaving teacher, is probably the only person in the ward who genuinely likes Len. This is because Len takes such care over the basket he is making. He spent ages getting the skeleton of his basket absolutely right. He puts Mango and me to shame. We've had to pull ours apart twice. Mrs Polidori was irritated because she doesn't like to waste the rattan. Just like 99 in the library she has limited supplies. After all, rattan doesn't grow on trees.

Len is meticulous as he weaves the strips of wet rattan. He can do fancy triple twists that hide the spokes of the basket, which Mrs Polidori tells us is a real skill. She instructs us to watch the craftsman at work, for he is surely the best basket-weaver she has ever seen in Ward 44.

Mrs Polidori is the official keeper of the scissors. If we need her to cut some rattan for us, we raise our hand and politely request her attention. If Len has his hand up, she will attend to him immediately, even though it may not be his turn. This is his reward for taking his basket seriously. It is Mrs Polidori's fervent hope that when he leaves, Len will continue making baskets. It is *our* fervent hope that Len merely leaves.

Now Len has a challenger. Anthea's basket starts promisingly with the binding of the spokes that will form the skeleton. Anthea works closely, never pulling the rattan too far from the work, which is the mistake that beginners usually make. Mrs Polidori watches Anthea in wonder and asks if she has done this before. Anthea says it is her first time, though Len doesn't believe her. He's used to first-time weavers being stupid and clumsy, making the sort of abominations that Mango and I make. He's suspicious of Anthea, and doesn't like it that Mrs Polidori has a new favourite. You can see the jealousy in his eyes. Anthea has done only three classes and caught up with Len. Mrs Polidori now asks us to watch *Anthea's* technique, so that we can learn to make proper baskets and not wicker disasters.

I wonder how long it will be before Len challenges Anthea to a wicker-off: a race against the clock to perform death-defying acts of quadruple and even quintuple twining, moves that only the brave or foolhardy would dare.

Under his breath, Len belittles Anthea's efforts. Her basket is the work of a show pony, a newcomer desperate for attention. Len predicts that Anthea's basket will last six months at most, then spring apart on the bus, probably catching a child in the eye. And does Anthea really think she will be able to carry anything of real substance in her basket? Six oranges, tops. That's all it will hold. If she thinks she can carry a couple of pineapples in this travesty of a basket, she'd better think again. Len is devious. He makes these comments under his breath. Mrs Polidori never hears. But the patients do. Anthea doesn't care. She makes furtive comments back and tells Len exactly where he can stick two pineapples.

Val says her basket is bad because she is an alcoholic. But neither Mango nor I are alcoholics, and our baskets are worse. I'll be very surprised if either of us leaves this hospital with a wicker receptacle of any kind. We stand next to Anthea and watch in awe. She likes it when we both watch. All it takes is concentration, she says. No wonder Mango and I are crap at baskets. But we are inspired now. We want to become experts at wickerwork. It's not so we can make baskets. We want to build a huge wicker man, then stick Len inside and set fire to it.

What is it about making a basket that is supposed to induce sanity? Most baskets are made in China, which should make it the sanest country in the world, yet they still melted all their saucepans when Chairman Mao told them to.

Later in the gym, Anthea throws the ball through the hoop again and again. She is utterly focussed.

Val does an exercise where she sits on a big inflated sphere known as a Swiss ball. She moves up and down on it, sometimes for a whole hour. What does she hope to achieve? Is it meant to reduce the size of her bum? If so, it isn't working.

Keith the bearded nurse is supervising the gym, and

he doesn't seem to have a problem with Val going up and down on the bright green ball. Apologetic Jill sits on an exercise bike but doesn't want to bother anyone by making a noise, so she pedals incredibly slowly. Keith doesn't seem to have a problem with this either. John, the Korean kid, does his own oriental exercises: slow trancelike movements that look elegant, though I can't see how they can improve his fitness.

Mango and I are at the end of a weight-lifting session. I have been slack again and it irritates Mango. He knows I can do better. This isn't stupid basket-weaving, he says. He doesn't want to be treated the way we treat Mrs Polidori. We are nice to her, we listen, and then we make baskets that even the least houseproud snake in India would be embarrassed to inhabit. We humans have just one body to protect us against the world, Mango says. We need to make ourselves as invincible as we can.

We do our post-workout stretches on the mat. Mango says it's important to stretch because after weight-lifting, muscles lactate. Stretching helps to get the lactation out. I'm sure this is wrong, but I don't question it. One of the stretches involves pushing our legs wide apart and looking at Anthea throwing hoops. She concentrates, holding her shooting arm up perfectly straight, never arching her back. It's hard to believe she doesn't know we are watching, but she doesn't turn our way. Maybe she is in a trance, like John. A netballer's trance.

'I am so in love with her,' Mango tells me. 'And she's good at pool.'

'Better than I am?'

'She concentrates.'

'So do I.'

'You could never be a professional pool player,' says Mango.

'Why not?'

'You had such a sweet shot all set up. You could've pocketed the yellow and the green, no problem, but instead you made your pants fall down.'

'True. But the thing is, Mango, if I had pocketed the yellow and the green, you would have forgotten about it ten minutes later. Everyone remembers when my pants fell down. I bet that years from now, people will still be talking about it.'

Len lies silent in the other bed. With any luck he has died. On the advice of Dr Vendra and Dr Maximew, I didn't take my medication tonight. I just pretended. I feel sharp-witted and awake. But I'm worried that my special lenses may not be working because I've yet to see any Nestorians. There is a snorting, rumbling noise. Len has started snoring and I have to accept the sad reality that he has not died. I leave my bed.

The vending machine in the corridor thinks it is so clever. What a wonderful piece of engineering it is, with its silver coils bearing chocolate bars and chips. You can have whatever you want by putting in your coins, pressing two buttons, then watching the coil magically turn so that your junk food falls into the tray below. When you reach for it, don't expect to grab anything you haven't paid for. The machine knows how to stop you doing that. If you put in too much money, the machine will give you change. If you don't put in enough, the machine won't give you anything, except return your coins, because the machine is honest.

The machine flashes little messages in red. *THE TIME IS 11.56 P.M. HAVE A NICE DAY.* But the machine is not as clever as I am, because I have a magic coin that it has never seen before. It has seen washers and other metal disks masquerading as coins. It knows all about them. But it doesn't know about my gold dollar coin with the fuse wire, which has fooled its brothers time and time again.

While I don't like any of the food in the machine, I know that I can put it to good use. I prepare to put my magic coin in the slot. Then I see something.

Two Nestorians are reflected in the machine's glass door. They're standing behind me. They hiss and snarl.

I've never seen them this close or this clearly before, and I'm afraid I'll piss myself. Then I remember what Dr Vendra and Dr Maximew told me. The recalcitrants can't harm me unless they are in groups of a hundred.

I check the reflection.

There are only two.

I have to be brave and face them, no matter how terrifying they are.

I turn quickly and yell out, 'Yahhhhh!'

They're gone. I creep down the corridors to see if there are any more. A human figure approaches. I realise I'm still holding the magic coin, which I must keep secret. I tuck it into my slipper.

'What are you doing?'

It's Keith, who is on night duty.

'Nothing,' I say.

'Did you make that noise before?'

'What noise?'

'You *did* make it, didn't you?' He sounds tired and not in the mood for games.

'I was having a nightmare,' I say.

'What did you put in your slipper?'

'Nothing.'

'Colin, please take off your slipper and show it to me.'

I take off the slipper. It has an insole, almost as if it is designed to conceal something. My magic coin is under the insole. I shake the slipper back and forth to prove that there's nothing there.

'Dr Parkinson doesn't want you wandering around at night,' he says. 'Would you like something to help you sleep?'

'No thank you.'

'Please go back to bed.'

'Sure. Sorry I made a noise.'

'That's all right. You can't help having bad dreams.'

'Good night, Keith.'

'Good night, Colin.'

My raid on the vending machine will have to wait. I go to bed but can't sleep. I've just seen two Nestorians up close. I shiver. Who's to say there aren't ninety-eight more somewhere in the ward?

CHAPTER 19

I wake up to the sound of a woman's scream. I'm horrified that I allowed myself to fall asleep, when I should have been vigilant. Worse still, I've *overslept*. Len is already up and about.

I get out of bed and walk down the corridor, where people are gathering. The scream, I learn, was made by Mrs Polidori. She swears she locked the big cupboard in the basket room. How could she forget such a fundamental thing? There is nothing valuable or dangerous there. The only sharp tool is the pair of scissors that Mrs Polidori brings to class. But somebody forced open the cupboard, pulled out the contents and threw them on the floor. The worst thing is that somebody has done a turd in Anthea's basket.

Val says it's the sickest thing she has ever seen. Jill bursts into tears. Anthea looks at Len, whose face bears no emotion whatever. Mango seems the most devastated of all.

I reach out to Anthea but she yanks her hand away and tells me she'd prefer not to be touched. Mrs Polidori is silent. She is wondering if she wants to keep working at a place where people use beautiful baskets for toilets. At last Len speaks.

'I think we all know who did this,' he says.

'Who?' asks Mango.

'Someone who knows how to pick a lock with a twisted paperclip.'

By now, people have heard about how I picked the lock on the drawer in the nurses' station. Some of the patients turn to me, as if I have betrayed them.

'It wasn't Colin,' says Mango.

'How do you know?' asks Len. 'Were you two in bed together all night?'

'It wasn't Colin,' says Mango, softly. 'It was you.'

Len is outraged. 'I don't know how to pick a lock.'

'It was you,' says Mango, almost whispering in Len's ear, 'and if you blame Colin, I will crack your skull.'

People shudder at the mention of violence.

'You can't talk to me like that,' says Len. 'We're supposed to help each other. I'll tell Dr Parkinson.'

Dr Parkinson has been attracted by the commotion. He looks into the room and shakes his head. He is disappointed in everyone, even himself, as if we are all responsible for this act of vandalism.

'The boy did it,' says Len.

But he does not have the support of the other patients. You can tell they think that he is the culprit. And of course he is. His jealousy of Anthea, with her basket-weaving expertise, is widely known. Len must have a paperclip of his own and he clearly knows how to use it. I wonder if Dr Parkinson realises that Len does not belong here. He is not helping anyone. He is upsetting people. He should be sent somewhere else, to the place where Grace and the angry man went. Or maybe they should give him ECT and turn up the voltage. He's got a piggy head. He'd probably smell like frying bacon.

'Colin, could you come to my office?' asks Dr Parkinson.

The other patients shuffle away, though Mango hangs back.

'Colin didn't do it,' he says. 'It was Len.'

Len looks the picture of innocence.

'And Len, I'd also like to speak to you later,' says Dr Parkinson.

Len says he's happy to assist Dr Parkinson in any way he can, always glad to be helpful. He's devious, like the Nestorians.

Dr Parkinson no longer looks boyish. It's as if recent events have aged him. He taps one of his pens on the desktop.

'Keith told me you were wandering last night,' he says.

'I was. A bit.'

'Why?'

'Len's snoring. I can't bear the snoring. I'd rather sleep on the pool table.'

'You've already made that joke.'

'It's the truth.'

'Keith saw you put something in your slipper.'

'That didn't happen.'

'He is convinced.'

'I showed him the empty slipper.'

'But you're good at making things vanish. You're good with a paperclip.'

'Dr Parkinson, I didn't break into the basket room.'

'You're going to tell me it was Len.'

'It was. Everyone knows he did it. The only thing he's good at is basket-weaving. And now Anthea comes along and she's better. He's got a grudge against her, just like he's got a grudge against me.'

'I'll speak with Len.'

'Make sure he tells the truth. Do you have a polygraph?'

'No, Colin. We don't use lie-detectors in Ward 44.'

'I guess you psychiatrists know when someone is lying.'

'Not always.'

I try an experiment. 'What if I told you that the shiny guys are real and not hallucinations? There really *are* beings from a parallel world and they are abducting humans. If I told you that, would you think I'm a liar?'

'No, I would be very worried and would reconsider the treatment you are currently receiving. Do you honestly believe the shiny guys are real?'

'No.'

'You'd tell me if you did?'

'Yes.'

'All right. We'll discuss this further in our next session.'

'Can I give you some advice, Dr Parkinson?'

He nods. 'If you want.'

'You should send Len away. He's wrecking everything. No one likes him. He might even be dangerous.'

'He isn't dangerous. I did the risk assessment myself. And other patients don't have a problem with him.'

'Oh, they do. People have stopped trusting one another.'

Dr Parkinson places his pen firmly in its caddy.

'And who started this? Who took the keycard? Who stole textbooks from my office?'

The force of Dr Parkinson's outburst surprises me.

'They were just books,' I say. 'You didn't even know they were missing.'

'You promised you wouldn't steal again.'

'I meant it.'

'Then where is the black texta? The one that was on my desk?'

'I don't know.'

Fortunately I'm not attached to a polygraph or it would explode. Dr Parkinson worries one of his grey curls with a finger. He is despairing, as though his dream of a perfect ward is unravelling like a badly made basket.

'If you only knew how much I care for you all,' he mutters.

'We care for you too, Dr Parkinson. But no one cares for Len. No one visits him.'

'His wife died recently.'

'That's supposed to make me feel sorry for him?'

'Yes, as a matter of fact it is.'

'His snoring probably killed her. How do you think he can snore so loudly and not wake himself up?'

'It's a medical mystery, Colin. Snorers never wake themselves up, no matter how loud they are.'

'I guess it's like ECT. No one knows why it works.'

'No one knows for sure.' Dr Parkinson gives another short nod. 'But it does work.'

'When you talk with Len,' I say, 'ask him what he can do with a paperclip. I bet he knows a few tricks.'

CHAPTER 20

Q. Anthea, I'm sorry about what happened.

A. . . .

Q. I thought you might want to talk about it.

A. What is there to say?

Q. How do you feel? It's all right to feel upset.

A. I hate this place.

Q. This is a very unusual occurrence.

A. Everyone in this place is *so* spastic. The people here are so old. How come?

Q. Colin and John are your age. Malcolm is only a little older.

A. John doesn't know English.

Q. He does.

A. Well, he pretends he doesn't. He won't talk.

Q. Maybe if you made an effort –

A. I shouldn't have to make a special effort. It's enough for me to say 'Hi' to him. If he doesn't answer, what am I supposed to do? I'm not his psychiatrist. I hate this place and everything about it.

Q. You're upset. It's perfectly understandable.

A. A disgusting old man crapped in my basket.

Q. We don't know who did it yet. But it was a disgusting act, yes.

A. Everything about this place is bad.

Q. Including me?

A. Yes.

Q. Why am I bad?

A. I don't like the way you hide things.

Q. How do you mean?

A. I don't know anything about you. All I know is you're called Dr Quayle and you're old.

Q. I'm forty-three.

A. That's the first time you've told me something about yourself. Are you married? Do you believe in God? How many kids do you have? Are you a lesbian? Ever gone skinny-dipping?

Q. None of that is important.

A. Of course it is. I'd like to know more about the person who's supposed to be helping me. Why don't I ask *you* some questions?

Q. What would you like to know?

A. Did you always want to be a psychiatrist?

Q. Yes.

A. Why?

Q. . . . I just . . . I always did.

A. When you were a very little girl, and the teacher asked what you wanted to be, did you tell her 'A psychiatrist?'

Q. Not when I was a *very* little girl.

A. What did you want to be then?

Q. Well, I wanted to be one of those ladies who work at the checkout of a supermarket.

A. Really? That was your dream?

Q. The checkout ladies always seemed so friendly and helpful.

A. I would die if my friends ever saw me working at the checkout of a supermarket.

Q. Why?

A. Would you be proud if your daughter was working at a checkout?

Q. I don't have any daughters, only sons.

A. Good. Now I know something else. And by the way, I don't know if you've noticed, but boys work at the checkout too. Would you be proud if your son was –

Q. They're eight-year-old twins. I would be very surprised to see either of them working at the checkout.

A. So you've got two little boys. Now I know a bit more about you, we can talk properly.

Q. We've been talking properly all along.

A. No, you've just been asking me a whole lot of dumb questions about my parents and my sister Carla and why I hate myself.

Q. Did you ring your parents yet? I know they're worried about you.

A. They prefer Carla.

Q. Why are you so convinced they prefer your sister?

A. Carla is everything I'm not. She's always been better than I am.

Q. How is she better?

A. She wins prizes at school. She's good at sport. She has good boyfriends.

Q. She's older than you –

A. By two years.

Q. Do you feel the need to compete with her?

A. I can't. So I decided to be a screw-up instead. Mum and Dad never like my boyfriends. But then, neither do I. I make bad choices.

Q. Deliberately?

A. You're the shrink. You tell me.

Q. Do you have a boyfriend now?

A. Not at the moment.

Q. Does Carla?

A. I don't know. She's overseas. She won some scholarship. Mum and Dad keep going on about it. Can we please stop talking about Carla?

Q. How are the shadows?

A. They don't bother me.

Q. But you still see them?

A. Hardly at all.

Q. Two or three times a day?

A. Less.

Q. I'm glad.

A. You don't look it.

Q. I think you're clinically depressed, Anthea. You've been depressed for a long time. Recreational drug use –

A. – is bad. I know.

Q. It may increase your depression.

A. And that's what the shadows are.

Q. I think so. Anti-depressants will help get rid of them.

A. How long will I need to take them?

Q. We'll see.

A. For the rest of my life?

Q. It's possible.

A. How depressing.

Q. Not really. A lot of people take anti-depressants. Even world leaders.

A. That doesn't exactly give me confidence.

Q. Good.

A. Good?

Q. Humour is a good sign. Have you made any friends?

A. Pardon?

Q. Here in the ward. Have you made any friends?

A. No. Well, maybe Colin. I think I like him.

Q. You told me you hate this place, and everything about it.

A. I hate *most* things about it.

Q. Then I believe you're making progress. I'm very sorry about your basket.

A. It's just a stupid basket.

Q. Have a good day.

A. You sounded just like a checkout lady then.

Q. And I've never been skinny-dipping.

A. Me neither.

CHAPTER 21

99 shakes her head in disbelief. Alcoholic Val has returned
The Secret Diary of Adrian Mole by Sue Townsend. To
keep her place in the book, Val turned down the corners
at the top of pages. The thing is, Val reads so slowly, no
more than a few pages at a time, that the first half of the
book is full of turned-down pages. She said she stopped
reading because she didn't like Adrian Mole measuring
his 'thing'. From her personal experience, it was nothing
like real life.

'How can someone do this to a beautiful hardback
book?' 99 says.

It's nothing new to her. 99 has an old book press
that she brought from home. It sits on the floor behind
her desk, a big horizontal vice for restoring warped
books to their original flatness. After smoothing out the
pages of *Adrian Mole*, 99 places it on the iron plate of
the book press. Then she winds the big handle on top,
which lowers the platen. It's delicate work. 99 knows

she can't lower the platen too much, or the book may break apart.

'It's the best we can do,' says 99, when she has the pressure just right. 'We'll never get rid of the creases, but at least someone else will be able to read it when it's flattened out.'

I like the way that 99 says 'we' as though she and I are a team.

I ask 99 if I can extend my loan on *The Castle*. It's taking me longer to read than I thought it would. 99 says she knows she can trust me, of course I can extend the loan. She wishes more people could be like Anthea and me. Anthea has already finished her vampire book, returned it in mint condition and is currently seeking another. She's here now, browsing the vampire department. Mango has followed her. He's desperate to be of help, though the library is unfamiliar territory for him. He wants Anthea to choose books that are high up, so he can reach for them. He wants her to choose heavy books so he can carry them. Most of all he wants her to be in love with him.

Anthea sees me. I don't want to interrupt. I'm hoping that after the shock of the morning, Mango can offer her comfort. It's best to put the image of Len crapping in a basket out of your mind as quickly as possible. But even though I want to leave Anthea and Mango alone, Anthea doesn't want that. It's not that she doesn't like Mango. I can see she does. But I think she likes it better when there are three of us.

We sit at the table together. Conversation isn't easy

because we don't want to relive the morning's events. I take the dollar from my slipper and do an elbow coin vanish. It's another simple trick. There's a move called a false pass, which is in a lot of coin tricks. Provided you can do the false pass well, you can entertain a lot of people. Anthea claps and 99 tells her not to.

Now Anthea wants to be the entertaining one. She remembers the fun she and I had with the remedial book about trucks. She picks up a book called *Our Animal Friends*. The first page has a picture of five ducks on a lake and two on the land. Anthea points to the caption, which informs us that ducks like to be on the water as well as on the land. She reads it aloud slowly. Mango looks on. I realise that Anthea is making a terrible mistake. She turns to the next page, which has a picture of two kittens playing and one sleeping. The caption informs us that kittens sometimes play and sometimes sleep. Once again, Anthea reads the caption slowly, in case we are unaware that kittens require sleep. Anthea doesn't understand why Mango and I aren't laughing. It was funny, she says, when I read the little-known fact that trucks travel on roads. I take the book from her and close it. Mango walks out of the library.

'Mango can't read very well,' I tell Anthea.

'Oh.'

'In fact, he'd probably have trouble with *Our Animal Friends*.'

'Right.'

'I'll put the books away, you find Mango and tell him – well, you can probably work out what to tell him.'

Anthea leaves and I put back the vampire books in their crypt. Eventually the curiosity overwhelms me. I go over to 99 and ask her what is so special about the last sentence in *The Castle* by Franz Kafka.

99 looks unsure of herself, like an amateur magician who is about to reveal the secret of a simple trick when she knows she shouldn't.

'There is no last sentence,' 99 says.

I can see she regrets saying it as soon as the words are out of her mouth.

'How can there be no sentence? That doesn't make sense.'

'There is only half a sentence.'

'What happened? Why didn't Kafka finish writing the book?'

'No one is sure.'

'What is the half-sentence? What does it say?'

'I've already given away far too much, Colin. You just have to finish reading *The Castle*. Don't read the last page until you have read the rest.'

'Why not?'

'Because if you do . . . your whole life will change. And it could be scary.'

'Seriously?'

99 whispers, 'Yes.'

My face must be a picture of confusion. 99 turns away but cannot keep a straight expression. She bursts out laughing. It's the first time I've ever heard her laugh. I'm on the receiving end of a practical joke. Usually it's the other way around. Doesn't 99 realise that some patients might believe her when she says things like that?

Len maintains that he's not guilty of basket-crapping and Dr Parkinson has given him the benefit of the doubt. Basket-weaving classes have been suspended because of the incident. The nurses tell us that we must not ostracise Len, because the culprit has not been identified. Since I'm the only other suspect, I resent the implication that I may be the basket-crapper. Val, ever the forgiving Christian, says that if Len *did* crap in Anthea's basket, it was probably by accident.

That evening in the recreation room, Len watches the news. He is in disgrace. The only person who sits with him is John. Anthea and Mango play pool. They don't like the news. I rarely watch it myself. The lead story is about a school bus that has run off an icy road somewhere in the Urals in Russia, leaving no survivors. For the first time in ages, John speaks.

'I wish I was on that bus,' he says.

'I wish you were on it too,' says Len.

Mango puts down his pool cue and wanders over to the chairs where the viewers sit. Len shies away. He is terrified that Mango will hurt him for wishing for something terrible to happen to John. But Mango walks past Len. He squats in front of John and takes both of John's small hands in his.

'Never wish for that,' Mango tells John. 'Promise me you will never wish for that again.'

John says nothing.

'Promise.'

When John gives his promise, Mango lets go of his hands and returns to the game. The story about the bus crash continues, even though it doesn't need to. We already know the facts. But there is some good film footage taken by a helicopter and the TV news wants to extract maximum value. Thank goodness apologetic Jill is not here. She'd probably think she caused the accident. Had she inadvertently left some ice on a road somewhere in the Urals in Russia?

Two figures stand outside the recreation room. I turn swiftly, expecting to see a pair of Nestorians. It's just a couple of humans, looking around nervously. They look relieved when Shamita joins them.

'Anthea, your parents have come to see you,' Shamita says.

CHAPTER 22

Even tho I dont understan a lot of wat Kolin say, I lik it wen he talk. No one else talk to me lik that. He dos not swer. Evryone at the trayning centr use to swer. It is v strange to be wit some one who dos not swer. It stop me swering to. And that is v good becos now Antha is heer and I kno that sum girls do not lik it when you swer evn if it is just shit. I want to talk lik Kolin.

I wish Antha wood look at me more and talk to me like Kolin talk to me. Her har is long and blak and her eyes are bron. Some times when I talk to her I kep lookin at her eyes and I cant here what she say. She probly think I am thik. I lov her since wen I fist see her and I hav told Kolin this.

Ther is some think els wich is v strange and I hav not told Kolin evn tho he say we mus hav no secret from each othr. Antha look a bit lik Kolin. Wen I see her shot barskets in th gym I notis this. Antha dos not look lik a boy and Kolin dos not look lik a girl, but they do look lik each othr. May be it is becos of the pajamas. But I wont tell docter partel this. We are stil talkin about th imposible cubbard and that is mor impotent. I stil hait th imposible cubbard and I stil drem about it. I wish I cood stop dremin about it and drem of Antha insted or evn Kolin but I just hav the cubbard.

CHAPTER 23

Anthea's parents look bland and are older than my parents. It doesn't seem possible that such plain people could produce such a striking daughter. They go with Anthea into the dining room, even though it's past eight o'clock and visiting hours are over. Since Anthea is a new patient, she is allowed to break this rule. I wonder if she will tell them about the incident in the basket-weaving group. I suspect she won't. It's a memory I couldn't bear. I'd bury it somewhere.

After speaking alone with her parents, Anthea wants to introduce them to Mango and me. She comes to fetch us from the recreation room. Maybe she thinks it will reassure her parents to see that there are normal patients in the ward who are her own age. I only hope that Mango doesn't put the grip on Anthea's mum. That would spoil the illusion. I quickly tell him we must not refer to each other as 'spazzo' and 'mental case'. We learn that Anthea's surname is Forrest, so her full name sounds like a place of mystery and romance: Anthea Forrest.

Mrs Forrest smiles nervously. She tells Mango and me she hopes we are making sure that Anthea is behaving herself. It's a joke she instantly regrets.

'Colin is magic,' says Anthea.

There is an awkward silence while Mr and Mrs Forrest work out if Anthea is mad for thinking that I am magic or if I'm mad for telling her that I am. I will have to do a parlour trick to show them what sort of magician I am.

I decide to do a snap vanish, which is simple enough. Mango and I are sitting together. Anthea is sitting with her parents on the other side of the dining table. Ideally the trick should be done for one person sitting directly in front of you. Sightlines are very important. If the person opposite you observes from an angle they can sometimes see how you do the trick, but I figure I'll get away with it. Mango knows how I do a snap vanish. Like most magic tricks it's so simple that to learn how it's done is a terrible anticlimax.

Placing the coin on the table, I pass my hands over it and click my fingers. On the third pass, I touch the coin with my middle finger as I click. It flies off the table so quickly that it seems to vanish. Of course, if the coin hits the floor, it will make a noise and the trick will be ruined, which is why people normally do it with a playing card. But Mango is my secret assistant. The coin flies off the table and lands in his lap. He will be discreet and remove the coin only when the audience is distracted and the excitement of the trick has passed.

I perform my click vanish and Anthea's mother smiles. She is relieved that her daughter is not mad, and that I merely know a few conjuring tricks.

'How do you do that?' Mrs Forrest asks. I realise there *is* a resemblance between mother and daughter. Will Anthea look like her mother when she grows old? Life can play cruel tricks.

'Colin is magic,' Anthea explains.

Mango backs her up.

Mr Forrest gazes about the room, as though he's a building inspector and not happy about what he sees.

'That's a false ceiling,' he says.

'Gary is a policeman,' Mrs Forrest explains. 'He notices things like that. It gets a bit tiresome.'

Mr Forrest does not look like a policeman. I can't imagine him in a uniform, carrying a gun or an electric police baton. All the other police officers I met have commanded respect. Maybe I'm just taken in by their severe blue outfits. If some bizarre cosmic force turned every policeman's uniform pink one day, we probably wouldn't revere them so much.

'Look at that brown patch in the corner,' Mr Forrest complains. 'There's a leak. And another. They should take the whole ceiling down, fix the leak then hang a new ceiling.'

This is not going to happen because Ward 44 is short of money. The fake ceiling will remain where it is and the brown stains will grow. The ceiling is like a magic trick, misleading people. But like all magic tricks, its secret is exposed when people look at it closely.

'I don't think Anthea wants to hear you talk about the ceiling,' says Mrs Forrest. 'I don't think any of us do, really.'

'I don't see the point of magic shows,' Mr Forrest says. Now he sounds like a policeman. 'When you see them on television, how do you know the magician isn't using a camera trick?'

'Colin isn't on television,' says Mrs Forrest, with forced calm. 'He's right here and he made a coin vanish.'

'It's in that boy's lap,' says Mr Forrest. 'He flicked it off the table and into that boy's lap. I would have thought that was painfully obvious.'

Mango looks as though Mr Forrest spotting the trick is somehow his fault. But it's mine, because I didn't pay attention to sightlines. Mango puts the coin on the table. Mrs Forrest and Anthea look disappointed. I don't know if it's because they think I've cheated them, or because Mr Forrest has made them seem dim or because deep down they want to believe in magic.

'Well, I still think it's clever,' says Mrs Forrest, trying to rescue the situation. 'And I would never have guessed how you did it.' She gives me a thin little smile.

'I'm sure you would have, given time,' says Mr Forrest.

'You didn't have to spoil it for everyone,' says Mrs Forrest. She realises she has spoken too sharply. 'He's being a policeman again.' She laughs.

'Colin can do other tricks,' says Anthea, desperate for me to prove that I really am much better than Mr Forrest thinks. 'Make a coin come out of Dad's nose.'

'No, I can't do that.'

'You can, I've seen you do it.'

'Your dad doesn't want me to take a coin out of his nose.'

Mr Forrest doesn't deny it.

'Is the food nice?' Mrs Forrest asks her daughter, eager to change the subject.

Anthea nods.

'So you're eating again?'

Anthea nods.

'Colin, you look like *you* could eat a bit more,' says Mrs Forrest.

'I'm naturally skinny,' I say. 'I can't help it.'

Mrs Forrest laughs loudly. 'I wouldn't be complaining about that if I were you. I would give anything to be naturally skinny. Malcolm, you're a big boy.'

'Thanks,' says Mango, who probably knows this already.

Shamita comes in, her dark face bearing an expression that is half sad.

'You will have to leave now,' she tells the Forrests. 'I'm afraid visiting hours are long over.'

'We're sorry we overstayed,' says Mrs Forrest, quickly rising to her feet.

'Please don't be sorry. It's lovely that you've come to visit Anthea. And you've met Mango and Colin as well, I see.'

'Mango?' Mr Forrest looks startled. 'You call that boy Mango?'

Shamita looks embarrassed. 'Malcolm. Sorry, I shouldn't have called him that.'

There is another awkward silence.

'You can make chutney out of mango,' says Mrs Forrest, brightly.

'I know,' says Shamita. 'I'm from India.'

'What's that got to do with mango chutney?' asks Mr Forrest.

'It's an Indian dish,' says Shamita, unruffled, even though Mr Forrest has spoken more harshly than he should have.

Mr Forrest stands. Anthea's parents give her a hug. Only now do I see how concerned they really are.

'You'll get better, won't you, princess?' Anthea's father says.

'And you'll ring us,' her mother says. 'They told me you can ring us whenever you like. I've brought you some coins for the payphone.'

Mrs Forrest fumbles in her purse.

'It's all right, Mrs Forrest,' says Shamita. 'We will give Anthea coins. Did you know that Colin can pull them out of people's ears and noses?' She smiles brightly.

'Yes, we know,' Mr Forrest says flatly.

Shamita is surprised that her funny remark gets such a subdued response.

'You get well too,' Mrs Forrest says to Mango and me. 'You seem like nice boys.'

'They are the best in the world,' says Shamita.

She escorts the Forrests out of the dining room, leaving the three of us looking up at the fake ceiling.

'Your parents are nice,' says Mango.

'Right,' Anthea deadpans.

'Really, you don't know how lucky you are.'

I explain to Anthea that Mango lost both his parents in a car wreck.

When we return to the recreation room we see that Len is watching TV alone. It's late. Len has the television volume up far too loud, probably to annoy the other patients.

'I don't want you here,' he says. 'I need to concentrate on this.'

He's watching a beauty pageant.

'You're an old perv,' says Mango.

'Oh, excuse me for being heterosexual,' says Len.

Shamita enters and asks Len to turn down the volume. He tells her to go back to bongo-bongo land. Rather than join Len as he ogles girls in swimsuits, Mango, Anthea and I say goodnight to one another and go to our beds. The girls in swimsuits don't really do it for me because they look cheap and fake, but I wonder what it would be like to share a bed with Anthea. I know that Mango is wondering this too.

THE TIME IS 11.56 P.M. HAVE A NICE DAY.

Once again I face the vending machine, which looks so confident in its impregnable shell. There are no Nestorians here tonight, no one but me, reflected in the glass door that protects the packets of chips and chocolate bars. Messages in red block letters scroll across an electronic slate in the top right-hand corner of the vending machine. *THIS MACHINE GIVES CHANGE.*

I decide which packets I need, then take out my magic

coin. There is a clinking noise to my right. Nestorians do not make this noise; at least, not in my experience. I steel myself for another close encounter with the invaders and spin around.

A man in uniform approaches, the keys on his belt rattling. He's a security guard. What is he doing here? We've never had a security guard here before.

'You're as bad as I am,' says the security guard. 'I can't walk past one of these machines without wasting my money on some piece of sugar wrapped in silver paper.'

I step away from the machine and palm my magic coin. The security guard looks friendly, despite the uniform.

'I reckon they should put carrots in these things,' he adds. 'Something healthy, so I don't get so fat.'

'The bags of nuts are probably healthy,' I say.

The security guard shakes his head. 'I have an allergy. One little peanut and the top of my head flies off. I have the same problem with prawns.'

'Then you're in luck. There aren't any prawns in the machine.'

The security guard laughs. He has a good laugh.

'Shouldn't you be in bed?' he asks.

'I can't sleep,' I say. 'The guy I share a room with has a snore that could frighten bears.'

He laughs again. 'My wife snores. That's why I work at night. Did you want something out of the machine?'

'I don't have enough money.'

'How much extra money do you need?'

I realise that this security guard is actually going to give me money.

'It's okay. It's probably not a good idea to eat chips at this time of night.'

The security guard nods. 'Do you feel like a cup of milk? I had a cup of coffee before and I saw there was plenty of milk in the fridge. How about we go to the dining room and get a cup of milk? What's your name?'

'I'm Colin.'

'Pleased to meet you, Colin. I'm Pete.'

'How come you're here?'

'Now, that doesn't sound very friendly, does it?'

'I'm sorry. I've never seen a security guard around here before.'

'It's my first night.'

I can't believe Dr Parkinson has gone to such lengths. He's rattled. It probably won't be long before we get the surveillance cameras.

'Have you ever worked in a hospital before?' I ask.

Pete nods. 'Sure.'

'A psychiatric hospital?'

Pete leans in close. His face has a mock-serious look. 'Is there anything I should know?'

'We're pretty harmless,' I say. 'There used to be a guy who was always angry.'

'I was told about him.'

'Who told you?'

'Keith. Our kids go to the same school.'

'Do you carry a gun?'

Pete laughs hard, then realises people are sleeping and he is being inconsiderate.

'No, Colin,' he whispers. 'I don't carry a gun.'

'What's that stick on your belt? Do you hit people with it?'

'I have never hit anyone with this stick.'

'Then why do you carry it?'

'You sound a bit paranoid. Oh. Am I allowed to say that?'

'It's okay,' I say.

Pete pretends to wipe sweat from his brow. 'I feel like a cup of milk. Care to join me?'

'I'm fine. I might just go back to bed.'

'I sure hope your friend isn't still snoring.'

'Oh, he's my enemy, not my friend.'

'I'm sorry to hear you talk like that, Colin. You seem like such a pleasant person. I try to like everyone. In fact I make a point of it. Well, good night, Colin. Don't eat too much junk food or you'll end up looking like me. Wouldn't that be a nightmare and a half?'

He laughs with restraint and walks away.

THIS MACHINE GIVES CHANGE. THE TIME IS 11.59 P.M. You're not going to rob me tonight. GO TO BED, YOU KLEPTO.

I'm lying in green grass. It should feel soft but it's hard, the way I imagine the grass on the teeing ground of a golf course feels. I wonder how I've come to be outside the hospital. It's still hard to open my eyes properly because of the lenses the Nestorians gave me. The world looks blurry, and it must be early in the morning because it's light but not warm. There's enough sunshine for me to see three flowers nearby: red, yellow and purple. Big round flowers that are nothing like the dreary ones that the visitors bring. I want to reach for one, but in my half-awake state I flounder.

At last I can open my eyes fully. I wipe away the gunk that has gathered. I gasp. Looking down at me are rows of cockroach faces. These are not friendly cockroaches like Dr Vendra and Dr Maximew. They do not have pleasant grasshopper eyes. The eyes are small and cold. These are the recalcitrants, the ones that have breached the infirmary – the ones I was warned about, and given lenses to see.

I sit up. There must be a hundred. They've come for me. I am not lying on the grass at all. There are no flowers. The cockroaches click with excitement.

'Colin, you have been misinformed,' the tallest cockroach says. 'There are certain matters you don't understand.'

I refuse to show that I'm frightened. 'Why don't you get it over with and abduct me?'

'You don't see the full picture.'

'Just take me,' I say. 'I *want* you to take me. I'll make things easier for you. I willingly offer myself. I want to be with the other humans you took.'

I surprise myself. I hadn't considered that I might secretly desire to be abducted by the bad guys.

'The humans who are abducted do not survive,' says the tallest cockroach. Others nod so that a sea of antennae moves up and down like a wave. 'Your kind ruined our world. We take from you what we require to live forever in *this* world. We take your senses – your eyes, ears, nose, mouth and hands – and we grow stronger by the day.'

'What do you do with our bodies when you have taken away our senses?'

The tall cockroach smiles. 'What do you think we do with leftovers?'

I'm horrified to think what might have happened to Briony and all the others. Were they dismembered? Eyes and ears pulled away? The sky brightens and the cockroaches look even more menacing. They extend their claws. I reach for a weapon, a sword. The cockroaches have no idea where it came from. They don't realise I'm magic. I smash the sword into the ground and make it sharper. I know that the cockroaches are not yet tangible in this dimension. My sword may not alarm them, but my determination does. They shy back as I slash and slash.

'Colin, it's me.'

The head cockroach produces a thin, shining weapon. It must be from Nestor or he wouldn't be able to hold it. He prods and it hurts me. I realise that *this* is what I must use against them. I drop my sword and grab at the weapon. The head cockroach struggles to keep hold of it, but I seize it from him.

'It's Pete.'

The other cockroaches are scared. I yell defiance and that frightens them more.

They will not take my eyes.

'Yaahhhhhh!'

I prod them with the weapon again and again, making it spark. There is electricity all around. I can smell it. The cockroaches are overwhelmed, screeching their terror as the voltage hits.

I hold my sword high and give a victory roar.

'Yaaaahhhhhhhhhhh!'

I've won. It hurts, but I've won.

CHAPTER 24

Dear Mr and Mrs Lapsley,

Further to my phone call I am writing to express my deepest regret about what occurred in the early hours of the morning.

Recently, Colin stole a keycard from the nurses' station. There have been a number of thefts lately. I took it on myself to improve security in the ward.

Mr Peter Tyler was hired after a rigorous interview and I believed him fit for the job. He will not continue his engagement with us. The device he accidentally used on Colin was an electric police baton, which administers only a minimal charge. I was not aware that Mr Tyler had the device.

According to Mr Tyler's report, he heard a noise coming from the recreation room. On investigation he saw Colin standing on the pool table, waving a pool cue. Mr Tyler suggested that Colin return to his room. Colin smashed the cue so that its end was sharp. He jumped from the table and ran towards Mr Tyler, who genuinely feared for his safety. Colin struck him, provoking Mr Tyler's defensive response with the baton.

I extend my sincerest apologies. Rest assured that Colin has not been harmed and is engaged in regular hospital activities as I write. Your manner on the phone was courteous and sympathetic, and I thank you for this.

We trust that you will continue to place your confidence in us and allow us to offer Colin the best possible treatment.

Kind regards,

Dr Joshua L Parkinson

CHAPTER 25

When I wake, I am in the room with Len and it's early morning. Len is asleep and silent. I feel a stinging sensation. I turn back the bedclothes, then pull down my pyjama pants so I can check the source of the stinging. On my right hip is a red mark in the shape of a crescent moon. I touch it and flinch. Then I smile. Last night I fought off the Nestorians. They screamed in agony, while I got away with nothing but a tiny burn. I was a hero then and I will be again.

My pyjamas are stale and I should change them. If I'm going to be a world hero I need to get my personal hygiene sorted out. Silently, so as not to wake Len, I take the clean pyjamas out of the cabinet beside the bed. Under the blanket, I take off my dirty pyjamas and change into the fresh ones.

'Are you going to the laundry?' asks Len. He startles me.

'Yes.'

'Take my pyjamas too.'

I can think of nothing worse than carrying Len's dirty pyjamas.

'Where's *The Castle*?' I say.

'What are you talking about?'

'There was a book in my cabinet, Len.'

'That's a poofy word.'

'"Book", "Cabinet" or "Len"?'

'I haven't been anywhere near your stupid cabinet. Take my pyjamas to the laundry.'

'No.'

'We are supposed to help each other, you bastard.'

'Why don't you help everyone by climbing into the tumble drier and suffocating?' I say.

'You've got no fugging manners, you poofter.' Len does a monstrous fart to emphasise his displeasure.

His basket rests safely beside his bed. Not for long, though, Len. Not for long.

When I walk by apologetic Jill's room I see that she is not in her bed. Maybe she's apologised herself out of existence? It's a shame. I like Jill and we haven't had the chance to know her properly.

The tumble driers are working. It seems they never stop. I put my pyjamas in the skip outside the laundry. It's too early for breakfast; I'm in no hurry. I wander into the laundry to see the big tumble driers full of our grey pyjamas, towels and other items. In the textile maelstrom I see some of the nurses' clothes. I open the door and the machine stops automatically. I take out pairs of jeans, jogging shorts, t-shirts. The jeans are small. They must belong to one of the nurses' kids. I figure the staff won't complain about their missing clothes, since they shouldn't be using the hospital laundry for non-hospital purposes. These clothes will come in handy for what I'm planning. I hide them under the vaulting horse in the gym.

Jill isn't in the dining room or the recreation room, and there's nowhere else she goes. I hope the Nestorians haven't abducted her. Maybe they did it before they came for me?

There's a new nurse at the station. She's probably about fifty. Her hair is black and curly; she has a broad smiling face and the biggest, most amazing breasts. Mango will absolutely love this new nurse. She speaks with an American accent that is playful and loud.

'What can we do for you, darlin'?' she asks.

'Hi,' I say. 'I'm Colin.'

'I'm Barbara. Aren't you handsome?'

I'm flustered. I don't like it when people tell lies about how I look. But I forgive Barbara because she is new.

'Do you know Jill?' I say. 'She's one of the patients.'

'She certainly is.' Barbara smiles. 'She is such a lovely person.'

'She isn't in the ward and I'm worried.'

'Oh. You don't have to worry about that,' says Barbara. 'Jill is on day leave. I signed her out myself.'

'What's day leave?' I ask.

'You don't know what day leave is?'

'I don't think so.'

'Oh. Well maybe I shouldn't have said anythin'. I'm sorry. I have a big mouth, don't I?'

'Is day leave when you get to leave the hospital?'

Barbara laughs. 'See, you *do* know what it is. You were just pullin' my leg.'

'Are you sure Jill will be okay? She thinks everything is her fault.'

Barbara nods sadly. 'Poor dear. How could anythin' be her fault? She's a sweetheart.'

'So how do you know she'll be okay?'

'Well, she'll be with her sister.'

'Her sister came to collect her?'

'Another gorgeous woman. It pains her so that Jill isn't well. They're goin' to spend the day together.'

'Was Jill dressed in her pyjamas?'

Barbara chuckles. 'No, darlin'. She was wearin' a very beautiful blue dress that made me quite jealous, I can tell you. Her sister brought it.'

'How can you be sure it was her sister?'

'She signed this form I have right in front of me, and she promised that she would bring Jill back by six o'clock.'

This puzzles me. 'I didn't know people could do that. Could someone take *me* out for a day?'

Barbara covers her mouth with both hands and rolls her eyes. Then she takes her hands away from her face. 'Colin, I have been the most dreadful chatterbox. I shouldn't be tellin' you these things. I'm very sorry. Why don't you just forget what I said? You can talk it over with your doctor. He's a lovely man. He'll have all the answers you need. And I look forward to gettin' to know you a whole lot better.'

'Thanks, Barbara.'

She leans towards me and speaks softly, like a best friend with a secret to share. As she does so, I smell her breath and realise that Barbara is a smoker, like Keith.

'Colin, I'm awfully flattered,' she says. 'You've been starin' at my bazoobies. I don't mind it one little bit, as you are such a handsome young man and I'm also exceedin' proud of my bazoobies. But some ladies *do* mind it, darlin', so you need to try really hard to look at their faces when they are speakin' to you. Now, don't be upset. Please don't. You were only doin' it when I was rattlin' on about what a blabbermouth I am, and frankly I talk so much that sometimes even *I* drift off and stare down at my own bazoobies to break the monotony.' Barbara laughs heartily at this.

I didn't know it was possible for patients to be taken out for the day and then returned, like a library book. Or maybe that's only for the *good* patients . . .

The smell of disinfectant in the dining room is especially strong. I find Mango and Anthea sitting together.

'Hello, spazzo,' says Mango.

'Hello, mental case,' I reply.

I sit next to Mango. Anthea eats only tiny amounts, with difficulty. Mango wolfs breakfast cereal and the milk runs down his chin. I eat nothing.

'Should you call each other spazzo and mental case?' Anthea asks.

'They are terms of respect,' I say.

'I think I should have a term of respect,' says Anthea. 'I'm sick of being called Anthea.'

'What do you want to be called?'

'Psycho,' suggests Anthea.

'No,' I say. 'It doesn't go with your eyes.'

'What about *the mental patient formerly known as Anthea*?'

I laugh. I don't think Mango gets the joke because he just continues eating. He pours milk on his second bowl of cereal, but he is impatient and pours too quickly. Milk splashes up, leaving drops on his pyjamas. It happens every morning. He doesn't like it when the milk lands on his pyjamas, but he hasn't learned how to make it stop happening. Shamita sets out the paper cups of tablets. Mango swallows them all at once, as if they are just another form of nourishment. Anthea has learned how to swallow her pills now. She drinks them down with water. I palm my tablets and merely pretend to take them. I've been doing this for two days. Or is it three? The days merge like meal cards.

News travels quickly in the ward. It must be the nurses chatting about things they shouldn't. By now, everyone in Ward 44 knows that Pete the new security guard burned me with a Hotshot. That's the name of the weapon that was used on me: an electric police baton. Dr Parkinson said he was sorry about the incident, and that Pete would not be returning to work. Val comes over to say she will pray for my recovery. I tell her it isn't necessary because it isn't that big a burn and God probably has more important things to do.

'How did it feel?' asks Mango, with his mouth full of cereal. 'When you got zapped?'

'I don't really remember.'

'Did it leave a mark?'

'Yes.'

'Show us,' says Mango.

'I'd rather not.'

'I want to see it too,' says *the mental patient formerly known as Anthea*.

'No.'

'How come you got zapped?' asks Mango.

'I don't know.'

I'll have to wait till I get Mango on his own to tell him that Pete was probably helping the Nestorians by supplying them with weapons. He may even be a Nestorian in human disguise. The recalcitrants are growing stronger if they are able to hold weapons. But I am strong too. At last I know how to fight them.

After breakfast, Mango suggests we go to the gym. Anthea says she can't because she has to see Dr Quayle. Mango is disappointed. But it means I will have a chance to tell him the truth about last night's confrontation, without Anthea overhearing.

Bench presses are Mango's favourite exercise. He puts four plates on either side of the bar, then does five sets of fifteen. I spot him, which means I have to stand at the end of the bench where he's lifting. Sometimes he can't manage to do the thirteenth or fourteenth lift so he yells out 'Spot!' and I grab hold of the bar and assist him with the lift. One of the new patients didn't know the rules of bench pressing. He heard Mango calling out 'Spot!' to me and thought that Spot must be my name. I had the name of a dog. The patient would call it out to me in the corridors, which was pretty funny, but Mango told him to stop.

It's hard to tell Mango about last night's confrontation because he's concentrating on bodybuilding.

'I was nearly abducted. There were hundreds of them,' I say. 'But I know how to fight them.'

'Good,' says Mango, between presses. 'It's important to know how to fight. You need to be stronger.'

Groaning, he pushes the bar one last time, then cradles it. He pants as I continue to tell him what I've discovered. I want him to be more excited.

'Electricity stops them,' I say. 'I turned the Hotshot on them and they ran.'

'You still need to be stronger,' Mango says. 'You have to learn how to defend yourself unarmed.'

'These guys come from another dimension. I can't just do judo on them. They've got two sets of arms. You do believe me about the Nestorians?'

'I will always believe you. It's your turn to do bench presses.'

I lie back. Mango insists I lift heavier weights. He keeps sneaking extra plates on either side of the bar. I tell him I won't be able to lift it, but he says things like 'No pain no gain,' and 'Remember to breathe.' As if I would forget.

We do the medicine ball sit-ups, a full set of a hundred. Again I notice that peculiar hook in the ceiling and wonder why it's there. Mango teaches me an exercise where we lie on our side on the gym mat, then push ourselves up on one outstretched arm, while keeping the rest of our body rigid. We hold the free arm up towards the ceiling, so we look like kites, and we hold this pose for a minute. Mango looks good as a kite, even though he is big and the position probably isn't very masculine. My supporting arm wobbles. Mango wants me to lift one of my legs while remaining in the kite position. I can't do it and I collapse on the gym mat.

'None of this is going to help me fight the Nestorians,' I tell Mango, quietly.

Mango gets out of the kite position and sits alongside me. 'It will,' he says.

I shake my head. 'We need electric weapons, like Hotshots.'

'Where are we going to find those?'

'This is a hospital. There must be heaps of stuff we could use. Like defibrillators.'

'What are they?'

'Those electric paddles they use on people when their heart stops. You see them on medical shows.'

'I don't watch medical shows.'

'Like this,' I say. I push my hands against Mango's chest and yell, 'Stat!'

'What does "Stat!" mean?'

'I don't know. People in medical shows yell it a lot, so it's obviously pretty important. We'll need two sets of defibrillators, one for you and one for me, so neither of us gets abducted.'

'You'll have to get a set for Anthea as well. I don't care if any of the others are abducted. Except maybe John.'

'Sure. I'll do my best. I've got a whole day to work on it. I think the abductions happen only at night.'

We head for the showers. There are three stalls. Inside each one is a bench where you put your clothes, towel and toilet bag, but the showers are so badly designed that everything gets wet unless you turn down the tap so low that nothing but a trickle comes out. Mango and I leave our pyjamas, underwear and towel on the hooks outside the stalls. We take our toilet bags into the stall with us since it doesn't matter if these get wet. I always take off my pyjamas and underwear really quickly then put the towel around me. As soon as the water is hot, I hang up the towel and step into the stall.

'Turn the shower off,' says Mango. He's naked and standing before the mirror.

'Pardon me?'

'Turn off the water. Take off your towel.'

'Why?'

'I want to see the mark the Hotshot made. I can't see it, so it must be under the towel.'

I take off the towel and stand naked in front of him. Mango looks at the red mark with a concerned expression. He has a scar from when his appendix was removed. The red-crescent moon shape is on the same part of my body. I wonder if I will have a Hotshot scar.

Mango frowns. 'Did it hurt?'

'I'm not sure.'

'Does it hurt now?'

'No.'

'Can I touch it?'

'Why?'

'Let me touch it.'

'Okay.'

Mango gently presses his fingers against the mark. He holds them there. Then he presses harder. I flinch.

'Sorry.' He takes his hand away.

'That's okay.'

'You're really injured.'

'No.'

'You are. I'm not going to let that happen again. Man, you're too skinny.'

'I can't help it.'

'You can. You're what they call a hard gainer. But you can build up.'

Mango turns back to the mirror. He clutches the cellulite where his six-pack used to be.

'Stand beside me,' he says. When I don't move, he adds, 'I am your personal trainer and you have to obey me.'

I stand beside Mango. His feet have hairs on some of the toes.

'Look in the mirror. Not at your feet,' he says.

'This feels gay.'

'Colin, I'm not gay. I just want to help you. There are some things you need to know. Look in the mirror. Feet aren't that interesting.'

I raise my head and observe myself. I can see ribs. There is an indentation at the bottom of my rib cage that looks especially ugly. It's not symmetrical.

'You need to be bigger,' says Mango.

'We have different body types. It's not possible.'

Mango shakes his head. 'I used to be like you, Colin. But I decided to make myself big. You have wide shoulders, so you're lucky. You can develop this muscle here, the trapezius. I'll point to mine. You point to yours. I want you to understand about muscles.'

Mango points to a muscle that makes his neck look big. I don't seem to have this muscle at all. I point to where I think it might be.

'Is this right?' I ask.

'A little higher. We are going to do weight exercises that will give you a big trapezius muscle. You'll look better in a t-shirt. I want your trapezius to be big like mine.'

'Okay.'

Mango continues his anatomy lesson.

'This is the deltoid. You point to yours.'

'There's nothing there.'

'Hold out your arm. That round shape on your shoulder is your deltoid. That's a really good muscle to build up. Guys with wide shoulders look good when they have big deltoids. I'll show you how to do that with dumbbells.'

'Do we have to do this naked?'

'Now, the pecs.'

Mango points to his pectoralis and I point to mine.

'You really need to work harder, Colin. Look how small your chest is. When we get out, I'm going to take you to a proper gym.'

Keith the bearded nurse wanders in to find us standing naked in front of the mirror. He frowns.

'What are you guys doing?'

'Playing with each other's dicks,' says Mango, who doesn't like Keith.

'He's kidding,' I say.

'Get in the showers,' Keith orders.

We step into our stalls and turn on the hot water.

'Maybe you shouldn't have said that,' I say.

Mango can't hear me. He sings a song that I've heard on the radio. I don't know what it's about and I'm pretty sure that he's mangling the words. Then I realise he's doing it because he wants me to laugh. The words he's singing are filthy and hilarious.

I laugh hard as the water pours down.

CHAPTER 26

A. Have you seen the picture of Jesus that Val has in her room?

Q. No.

A. It's three-dimensional and it blinks when you walk by. Only I don't think Val knows that. Once she came into the room and found me leaning one way, then another. Jesus was fluttering his eyes at me. Val asked me what I was doing. I said I was looking at blinking Jesus. She told me not to use the Lord's name in vain.

Q. Quite.

A. *Quite?* I thought I was being engaging. Isn't that what you want? You psychiatrists are never happy.

Q. Anthea, it doesn't help anyone if you make up things.

A. I didn't make that up. It happened.

Q. You haven't been truthful with me. I spoke with your parents.

A. You went behind my back. I thought you weren't going to do that.

Q. I needed to ask them something. It was important.

A. I can't believe you went behind my back.

Q. You don't have a sister called Carla.

A. I do.

Q. You're an only child. There is no Carla.

A. But I fooled you, didn't I?

Q. Why did you make her up?

A. Guess.

Q. I'd prefer you to tell me.

A. . . .

Q. Have you mentioned Carla to anyone else?

A. No. I invented her the first time we spoke.

Q. You were very convincing.

A. Thank you.

Q. Were you trying to test me?

A. What do *you* think?

Q. I'm not sure.

A. I'm a screw-up. We do things like that. It's no big deal. I often make things up.

Q. You have to stop doing it. Have you told me other lies?

A. None.

Q. Anthea, I want to help you cope with the shadows. I can't do that unless you're completely honest.

A. Okay.

Q. I'm serious.

A. Okay. I'm sorry.

CHAPTER 27

As Tim accompanies me to the building next door, I tell him that *The Castle* by Franz Kafka is missing. I will need a new book. Does Tim have any recommendations? He has good taste, I tell him. I want him to talk and joke, like he usually does. After all, Tim is everyone's favourite nurse. I think Anthea may even fancy him, but I'll continue trying to matchmake her with Mango, because I know how much he wants that.

Tim does not want to talk about books. As we walk down endless corridors and climb stairs, I comment that the architect must be MC Escher, the artist who does etchings of buildings that are optical illusions. At first they look normal, then you realise they are impossible. (I mentioned MC Escher to Mango once and he thought he was a rapper. I told him that's exactly what he was.)

Tim doesn't want to talk about MC Escher. He is withdrawn. I want to tell him a joke, but I can't think of a good one. And I can't do a magic trick because we're walking.

'Keith's been fired,' says Tim at last. 'He has to leave in two days' time, at the end of the week.'

'I'm sorry about that,' I say.

'Dr Parkinson thinks Keith's responsible for what happened to you. He was on night duty. Shamita was supposed to be there but she was sick and Keith wasn't at the station.'

'He was probably outside having a smoke,' I say.

'How would you know? You were sleeping on the pool table.'

I realise that Tim is upset because of *me*. He thinks it's my fault that Keith has to go.

'I'm sorry, Tim, I didn't know you liked Keith so much.'

I wonder if Tim might even be in love with Keith and that's why he's so mad with me. If this is the case, I will take back my remark about him having good taste.

'He's only human,' says Tim. 'They work us too hard. So what if he has a smoke from time to time?'

I worry that there will no longer be a smoking nurse in Ward 44, which means the door downstairs will not be propped open. I'd been counting on that, in the event of my needing an escape route one day. More importantly, I worry that I have made an enemy of Tim.

We reach Dr Vendra's office. Dr Vendra is wearing his impeccably dressed man disguise again. He smiles his disarming smile.

'Colin, it is good to see you again.'

Tim closes the door and leaves. I hear his footsteps recede in the corridor. Dr Vendra's human disguise instantly falls from him in a shower of scales. As he sheds the disguise I look around the office. The picture on the wall has changed. It's now a Dutch landscape featuring a flood. Peasants are struggling to remain afloat, only to be dissected by the blades of homicidal windmills.

'You changed the picture,' I say.

'Actually, *you* did,' Dr Vendra replies.

'But you said it wouldn't happen. There'd be no flood, the windmills wouldn't attack.'

'I said it wasn't *likely* to happen. There is a difference.'

I feel uncomfortable and eager to leave this place. But the third door, the door to the infirmary, hasn't appeared yet. There is merely a blank wall. His human costume fully gone, Dr Vendra is revealed in all his Nestorian glory. He tells me to look into his gaze and not at the wall. Last time he did this, he was a human with intense eyes. Now he is a giant cockroach with big round ones that are bright red and mirrored, like a grasshopper's eyes in colour-negative. If I had first encountered Dr Vendra when he looked like this, I would have run screaming from the room.

At last the third door to the infirmary appears in the wall. I know I shouldn't touch it because it's too hot for humans. Dr Vendra obliges and opens it with ease.

This time Dr Vendra has better luck with the infirmary and we are delivered closer to the building with the melted doors. The Nestor light is cold sodium and no one is around. I rub my upper arm, which stings again.

'It will soon be rush hour,' says Dr Vendra. 'Let's make haste.'

I picture hundreds of cockroaches streaming onto the concourse and immediately follow Dr Vendra.

'My arm hurts,' I tell him.

'Be glad you don't have four,' he replies.

One of the commuter shuttles drifts silently overhead, producing clouds in its wake. It wobbles, as if buffeted by wind, but there is no wind on Nestor. I stop to observe.

'We don't have time,' Dr Vendra insists.

The shuttle judders, and loses altitude. There is something wrong. If it does not change its present course it won't make the landing on top of the building. It will crash into the side, like that bomber plane that flew into the Empire State Building.

'Come with me,' Dr Vendra says, seemingly unconcerned about the imminent crash.

'There's going to be an accident,' I say.

'It's a strong building,' says Dr Vendra. 'It won't be damaged.'

'What about the shuttle?'

'See, it's changing course. All will be well.'

But all is not well. In an effort to avoid collision, the shuttle banks sharply to the right. Its hull clears the corner of the building, but its altitude continues to drop. The shuttle is in free fall. Dr Vendra seems more concerned about our own safety and tries to pull me away. I stand my ground and wonder how many Nestorians are on board. The shuttle looks large enough to accommodate at least two hundred.

'Colin, we can't do anything for them,' Dr Vendra says.

'We must.'

'No, the shuttle left the path. There are designated shuttle lanes. If citizens only obeyed the rules, things like this wouldn't happen.'

The shuttle strikes the concourse with a muted thump. I duck instinctively and close my eyes, as if there might be an explosion, and scattering of debris. When I open my eyes again I see that there is little more than a crack in the vehicle's side. It sits at an ungainly angle. Otherwise it's undamaged. The shuttles must be built from a material that is almost indestructible.

'You see?' says Dr Vendra. 'Nobody is harmed.'

The crack in the hull opens wider, and red shapes emerge. It's not easy for them. They move with effort, as though they're in pain. Six Nestorians manage to emerge from the crashed shuttle, their legs shaking. They are definitely injured. I move towards them, to see if I can assist. But Dr Vendra holds me back.

'Colin, our time is limited. There's nothing we can do. Please, the future of both our worlds is at stake. I cannot allow you to jeopardise the mission.'

'We can't just leave them.'

'We can.'

'These are your people. They aren't the evil recalcitrants. They're just innocent Nestorians on their way to work. Don't you feel anything?'

'They left the path. I'm afraid they have brought their fate upon themselves.'

One of the six Nestorians collapses, his bandy cock-roach legs no longer able to support him. He lies on his back with legs and arms flailing. I feel sorry for him. But Dr Vendra pulls me back with a gentle claw.

'It's a tragedy,' Dr Vendra tells me, 'but we can do nothing about it.'

'I hate you for not wanting to help them,' I say.

For the first time, Dr Vendra looks angry. 'Colin, do you know anything about Nestorian medicine?'

'No.'

'Exactly.'

'But there might be *something* we can do.'

'There are other, more qualified people.'

'You're a doctor.'

'It's been a long time since I tied a tourniquet.'

Two small vehicles arrive at the scene of the accident. They are white boxes on wheels, and each has a vivid red cross painted on the side. It's interesting that the symbol for first aid is the same here as it is on earth. Nestorians clamber from the boxes to lend whatever assistance they can.

'You see? Help is at hand.'

'I just don't like walking away.'

'It's a question of priorities. I'm very upset that you said you hate me, Colin, especially when Dr Maximew and I have made such an effort to help you.'

'Okay, I don't really hate you. There are a lot of things about this planet I don't understand.'

'I don't hate you either, Colin. I don't know how anyone could.'

As we climb the crumbling stairs, Dr Vendra tells me some good news. He and Dr Maximew believe they have located the abducted humans. And contrary to what the recalcitrants told me, the humans are safe and alive. I forget about the crash I've just witnessed. It lifts my spirits to hear such good news. I'm so overwhelmed that I misjudge what level we're on, and push the door on the landing. It's stiff, but it starts to open. I then notice the number eight on the door and cease pushing. I've made a mistake. I ask why Dr Vendra and Dr Maximew work on the ninth floor when it's so difficult to climb the stairs. What's wrong with the ground floor, or maybe the very top floor where the shuttles land? Dr Vendra ponders before answering.

'We can hardly expect a building that has stood for thousands of years to be fully sound. Some regions are uninhabitable, even by us.'

'I guess I should mind my own business.'

'You are our guest and may ask whatever you like.'

'Why does the door open if the eighth floor is uninhabitable?'

Dr Vendra doesn't respond. I may be able to ask what I like, but it doesn't mean I will get answers.

'We are running terribly late,' says Dr Vendra. 'Dr Maximew may be terse with me. I do dislike it when he's terse. To the ninth floor, Colin.'

We emerge on the ninth floor, with its low ceiling and grimy walls. We reach the correct door. Dr Vendra pushes it open and I see Dr Maximew with his back to us, as he gazes out of the window. He is no doubt looking down at the crashed shuttle. It makes me wonder if Dr Maximew has family. Does he have a wife and some little cockroaches at home? Dr Maximew replaces the paper screen on the window and turns, his antennae twisting with excitement. If the crash has upset him, he does not show it.

'Colin, I can't tell you what a pleasure it is to see you,' says Dr Maximew. 'Would you like some water?'

There is a full cup on the desk. I drink some and screw up my face. The water has changed taste again. It has a strong, acrid smell.

'Is this urine?' I ask.

'We are not in the habit of serving our guests urine,' says Dr Maximew. 'Unless, of course, they request it. Has Dr Vendra told you the good news?'

'You mean, about the abducted humans?' I say.

Dr Maximew is greatly excited. 'They have been located,' he says.

'Where?'

'You will see.'

'Are they okay?'

'You will see.'

'Is Briony there?'

'All in good time. But you too have some wonderful news, I think. Please tell us. You are our guest and must speak first.'

I'm so preoccupied by the thought of seeing Briony that I don't hear properly.

Dr Maximew prompts me. 'Well? Is it true that you've found a weapon to use against the recalcitrants?'

I'm thrown. 'How did you know that? Can you see me when I'm on earth?'

'Sadly, we cannot.'

'Then you can read my thoughts?'

'You make it difficult for us. Yours is a complex mind. But we do pick up the odd vibration. Tell us what you have discovered. Then we shall move on to other matters.'

I take a deep breath, knowing I will not find out more about Briony until I tell the doctors what they want to know.

'I think I've worked out how to stop the recalcitrants from abducting humans,' I say.

Dr Maximew and Dr Vendra exchange joyous looks. 'We knew it. There is a weapon?'

'I found out by accident. I didn't really study the problem or anything like that.'

'You are modest,' says Dr Vendra. 'I'm sure the problem was foremost in your mind. Tell us what you have learned.'

'There's no electricity in this world,' I say.

The doctors nod sadly.

'We have never developed an efficient means of generating it,' says Dr Maximew. 'Water is scarce. Hydroelectricity is out of the question.'

'Our air is still,' adds Dr Vendra, 'so we cannot generate electricity from the wind.'

'Solar energy is likewise impossible.'

'And nuclear power hasn't been attempted because of the apocalypse. It's considered to be in bad taste.'

'Perhaps we should allow Colin to speak,' suggests Dr Maximew, gently placing a claw on Dr Vendra's forearm.

'On earth we have these things called electric police batons,' I explain. 'They give people shocks.'

'How barbaric.' Dr Maximew shudders.

'Last night, the Nestorians came for me. I could see a hundred, thanks to the lenses.'

Dr Maximew and Dr Vendra throw up four sets of forearms in horror.

'But I was okay,' I reassure them. 'I fended them off with an electric weapon.'

They lower their forearms in relief.

'How did you get such a weapon?' asks Dr Maximew.

'A security guard gave it to the Nestorians. The guard might even have been a Nestorian in human disguise. I'm not sure.'

Dr Maximew scratches his carapace. 'And you wrested this weapon from the grasp of the recalcitrants?'

'Yes.'

'How could they hold it?'

'I think they are growing stronger.'

'We were afraid of this,' says Dr Maximew.

'But I know how to stop them. Do you have more of those contact lenses?'

Dr Maximew shakes his head. 'We lack the funds.'

'But we have the greatest confidence in you, Colin,' says Dr Vendra.

'What about the abducted humans?' I ask. 'Are they okay? Do they have eyes, ears, noses, mouths and hands?'

'Yes, Colin, they are alive,' says Dr Maximew.

'Can we see them?'

Dr Maximew scratches the hairs on his forearm. I've learned that this is what Nestorians do when contemplating a tricky question.

'Unfortunately, the abducted humans are on the far side of Nestor. It would take a long time to get there, and the situation is urgent. We'll show it to you in pictures instead.'

Dr Vendra and Dr Maximew charge up their antennae and place them to my forehead.

Colours spin and it takes at least a minute before I get a clear picture. I'm flying, but the terrain has changed. This is the far side of Nestor, and it's hard to believe that it's the same planet. I thought that the nuclear war had destroyed everything, but on this side of Nestor there are hills covered in dark trees. They don't look welcoming. The abducted humans would be frightened to be left in a place like this. I hate to think of how Briony must feel. I swoop out of a grey sky and find myself below the treetops in a dim, forbidding place. The ground looks like thick black mud.

I estimate that I'm three metres above ground, floating through alien vegetation that is savage and poisonous. I see a man. He doesn't look like a frightened abductee. On the contrary, he is arrogant and menacing. The man wears a red leather jacket and large mirrored sunglasses that hide half his face. There is no harsh sunlight in the forest. He doesn't need to wear sunglasses. His age could be anything from thirty to fifty years. The red leather jacket makes it hard to tell. There is a bulge in one of the jacket pockets. Although I don't see it, I sense that there is a weapon there. The man takes off his glasses so I get a clear view of his face.

I gasp and lift my arms. The image flares a burning white. And I'm suddenly being transported to another part of Nestor. I prepare for a change of perspective. But when the image comes back it is not so different. Fierce plants with long spikes grow in dense clumps. Then I hear a familiar human voice. I nearly cry when I recognise it.

'Will we get into trouble?'

It's Briony. She's nearby. I wish I could see her.

'Where did you come from?' says Briony's voice. 'Were you in the forest?'

A man's voice says, 'I'm a park ranger.'

'You don't look like a park ranger,' says Briony's voice. 'Why are you wearing sunglasses? And your shoes are strange.'

'They're made of canvas,' the man's voice replies. 'I wear them so as not to squash the beetles. A park ranger has to be careful about things like that. And I wear the jacket to protect me from thorns.'

After a few seconds, I hear Briony's voice again.

'Have we done something wrong?'

I dart about under the thick canopy of trees, trying to find Briony, but the image breaks up. I move slowly to restore it.

'When you're in a national park you shouldn't move logs,' says the man's voice. 'It upsets the animals that

live there. You won't get into trouble. I won't report you.
But you have to come with me.'

I hear a third unfamiliar voice.

'We don't want to come with you.' It's a boy.

'*You* can stay,' says the man's voice. 'But your sister
has to come.'

The boy speaks again. 'Where are you going to take
her?'

'Just stay here. We won't be gone long.'

'You can't take her into the forest. I won't let you.'
The boy sounds weak. His voice wavers. 'I'll stop you.
I will.'

Briony's voice cries out words I can't hear, as if I'm
underwater. Then there's silence, black and cold.

Dr Vendra and Dr Maximew are tending to me in the
gloomy office. Dr Maximew is wiping the goo from my
forehead, the slime that Nestorians secrete from their
antennae.

'Briony was there,' I say. 'But I didn't see her.'

'Just relax,' says Dr Vendra.

'I think she was in danger. I need to see the pictures
again.'

Dr Maximew stops wiping my forehead. 'We can't do
that,' he says.

'You have exhausted us,' says Dr Vendra.

'Why do you think Briony was in danger?' says Dr
Maximew.

'I heard a human voice.'

'The Nestorians are the true enemy,' says Dr Vendra.
'If you didn't see or hear them, Briony is safe.'

I should feel relieved, but I don't. 'When will I see her?'

'Next time.'

'But –'

'Next time. We give you our word. You have to trust us.'

Dr Vendra leads me from the office. In the corridor, he taps on door after door, trying to find the right one. I hold out my hand and touch the door nearest me. It's warm like pyjamas fresh out of the dryer.

'I've found the portal,' I say.

'You're very gifted, Colin,' says Dr Vendra. 'We were right to put our faith in you. The recalcitrant Nestorians are spreading all over the earth. Fight the good fight. Escape from Ward 44. Find weapons.'

CHAPTER 28

I wake up with a pain in the chest and again it's hard to
open my eyes. I wonder if I will ever get used to the contact lenses the Nestorians gave me. I touch my forehead
and wipe away a residue of cockroach slime. The room
is hot. It feels like noon. Len is not in the bed opposite.

Loud yells are coming from the direction of the
nurses' station. I hear Mango. I get out of bed and run
down the corridor, which is against the rules.

Mango is clinging hard to Keith, the bearded nurse
that I have caused to be sacked. Even though Keith
knows about Mango's condition, he's swearing and calling him names. Mango is sub-human, he yells, a moron.
It's an unending torrent of abuse from the man whose
job it was to be sympathetic. Because Keith is so loud,
Mango has to yell back. He doesn't swear. He doesn't
threaten. He simply tells him that he wants to let go
but can't. He wants Keith to stop saying terrible things.
I join a small group of patients who are appalled by

Keith's behaviour. Mango's face is full of despair. His eyes are closed and watering. He's never tried harder to let go of someone.

Shamita is appalled by what she sees. She is shouting at Keith to stop mistreating the patient. Tim has a sedative shot for Mango. But Keith writhes so hard that Mango's huge body is tossed about. Tim orders Keith to stop moving. He's being a bloody disgrace, Tim says. I was wrong about Tim. He's certainly not in love with Keith. He crouches and yells to Keith that if he doesn't keep still, he will stab him with the needle. I've never heard Tim speak with such venom in his voice.

Keith stops thrashing.

'Mango,' Tim says gently, 'can you relax your arm just a little?'

'No,' says Mango, gritting his teeth.

'Then I'm sorry.'

Tim pulls down Mango's pyjama pants. His backside is big and white. Tim jabs with the needle then pulls the pyjama pants back. As the sedative takes effect, Keith works his way free. He realises he is now the most hated person in the ward, even more despised than Len. He skulks away, knowing this is the last time he will see any of us.

Dr Parkinson is slow to arrive at the scene. He looks tired and defeated, no longer a leader. He seems almost as lost as the rest of us.

'Next time you sack someone, do it properly,' snarls Tim, who remains crouched alongside Mango. 'You sack them, they leave immediately.'

It's brave of Tim to speak like this. All Dr Parkinson does is ask Tim to fetch a gurney.

'Please, go back to your rooms,' says Dr Parkinson, quietly.

But only four of the patients leave.

'Shamita, attend to the patients.'

Tim arrives with the gurney as Shamita breaks up the gathering. Tim and Dr Parkinson move Mango onto the trolley and wheel him to his room. Anthea and I exchange glances. We follow, as Mango is led away. Dr Parkinson notices.

'Please, leave us,' Dr Parkinson says. 'Anthea, you should be with Dr Quayle. Go to your appointment.'

Anthea leaves but I remain.

Dr Parkinson frowns.

'Colin, go to my office.'

'It isn't my appointment yet, Dr Parkinson. I'm not going away.'

Dr Parkinson, too tired to argue, continues pushing the gurney and I tag along.

Mango comes around about half an hour later to see me sitting at the foot of his bed. I stand when he speaks.

'What time is it?'

'Just after ten o'clock,' I say.

'How long was I asleep?'

'Thirty minutes or so. Tim had to give you a sedative. You're still groggy.'

'Where's Anthea?'

'She had to see her doctor.'

'She sees her doctor a lot.'

'Too much, I reckon.'

Mango sits up and rubs his arm. 'It doesn't feel sore. Where did Tim inject me?'

'I'll give you three guesses.'

Mango feels his backside and looks pained.

'Oh, man, did Anthea see?'

'Not that much.'

'Why did he have to jab me in the arse?'

'I guess because you were straining the muscles in your arm. Especially the bicep.'

Mango yawns. 'I should get up.'

'Lean on me, if you like. You'll be wobbly.'

'I wish Anthea had stayed.'

'Dr Parkinson sent her away.'

'How come he didn't send *you* away?'

'Because I wouldn't let him.'

Mango tries to stand, but he's still too groggy. He swings back into bed. 'Maybe I'll stay here a little longer.'

Now that no one else is around, I can deliver my bombshell.

'I'm planning an escape,' I say. 'We have to get out of here. The Nestorians are growing stronger. We have to find weapons and stop them.'

'Okay.'

Mango doesn't sound committed, probably because of the sedative.

'I've been working on an escape plan. I knew something like this would happen.'

'You're good with plans. What about the cupboard?'

'What?'

'If I escape with you, we have to look for the impossible cupboard.'

'We will,' I promise. 'We'll fight the recalcitrants and we'll find the impossible cupboard.'

'And Anthea has to come with us,' says Mango.

'Anthea?'

'If we escape, Anthea has to as well.'

I consider this. Will Anthea be a liability? Will she reveal our plan to the staff? I don't know if I can trust her. Then I see how much Mango needs Anthea to come along.

'We'll take Anthea with us. If she wants to come,' I say.

'She'll be able to help,' says Mango. 'She's smart, like you.'

I just nod.

'And her dad's a policeman,' says Mango, before drifting off.

I've been missing the obvious. Her dad's a policeman. *Of course* Anthea will be able to help us.

Tim enters.

'Just checking on Sleeping Beauty,' he says, smiling.

'He's okay,' I say. 'He was awake for a bit, then he fell asleep again.'

'Did you find your copy of *The Castle*?'

'Not yet,' I say. 'I think Len stole it.'

'Len is being blamed for a lot of things. Why would he steal your library book?'

'Because he knows I like it.'

'I'm sure it'll turn up,' says Tim. 'And when it does, you mustn't read the last sentence before you finish the book.'

'You mean half-sentence,' I say.

Tim is crestfallen. 'Somebody told you?'

'99 did.'

'Who's 99?'

'The librarian,' I say, realising I don't know her real name.

'Cleopatra,' says Tim.

'Her name is Cleopatra?'

'No. Some of the staff call her that because of her hair. Oh, I think I understand why you call her 99.'

'Anyway, she didn't tell me what the half-sentence is. So it's still a secret.'

Tim looks at the floor. 'I was rude to you before,' he says. 'I was annoyed about Keith being sacked because we all work so hard and I thought it was unfair. I also thought that having a security guard around the place was a stupid idea. I was angry when I snapped at you for sleeping on the pool table. I'm sorry. But please don't do it again.'

'Why did Keith hate Mango so much?' I ask.

'He didn't hate Mango. He had come to the end of his tether. Even psychiatric nurses lose it sometimes. It's hard to be a nurse.' Then Tim chuckles. '99. You're right. She does look like Barbara Feldon.'

I notice that Dr Parkinson has stubble. This is a new experience for him and he can't leave it alone. He cradles his chin and rubs the bristles along his jawline with an index finger. I don't know if Dr Parkinson is trying a new look, or if he's simply not made time to shave. He looks sleepy.

'Are you all right, Dr Parkinson? I could come back later, if you like.'

'No, no. This is your session. I'd like to talk.'

'What will we talk about?'

'How are the hallucinations?'

'Gone,' I say.

Dr Parkinson raises his eyebrow. 'Really?'

'Completely.'

'How long has it been since you last saw them?'

'Do you remember our last session?'

'Yes.' Dr Parkinson checks my folder on the desk.

'Well, I never saw them again after that. You must be a very good psychiatrist. So I'd say I'm ready to leave.'

'I don't think so, Colin.'

'Oh.'

'Sorry.'

'What would stop me walking out the front door right now?'

'Do you plan on doing that?'

'No, but just say I did?'

'In your pyjamas?'

'Let's say I had normal clothes.'

'Well, you'd have to discharge yourself, and you couldn't do that without a clean bill of health from me.'

'The nurses would stop me leaving?'

'Yes, they would. For your own good.'

I nod. 'That's reassuring. Did you know that your pencil is made of rubber?'

'Sorry?'

'Watch this.'

I hold Dr Parkinson's pencil between my thumb and index finger, about three quarters of the way down its length. Then I loosen my wrist, and shake the pencil fluidly up and down. It's a very basic optical illusion.

'See? Rubber pencil.'

'Could I have it back please?'

'Don't you think it looks like it's made from rubber?'

'No.'

'Oh.' I'm disappointed. I'm obviously not doing the trick right. I used to do it for Briony and she would fall for it. But then, it's probably easier to fool an eleven-year-old girl than it is to fool a psychiatrist. I hand back the pencil.

'Can I ask a question?' I say.

'Of course.' Dr Parkinson shakes the pencil, to see if *he* can make it look like rubber.

'Are there any defibrillators in this ward?'

'Yes, we have defibrillators.'

'Where do you keep them? Could I borrow some?'

Dr Parkinson closes his eyes and wipes his face.

'No, Colin,' he says. 'You can't borrow any defibrillators. What on earth do you want them for?'

'Just a practical joke.'

'I don't understand.'

'Dr Parkinson, what did you mean before when you said that jokes are important to me?'

'Did I say that?'

'In another session. It concerns me that you don't remember.'

'Well, I think that jokes are your way of coping.'

'With what?'

'You'd be surprised how many comedians suffer depression. Being funny is their way of dealing with it.'

'You still think I have depression?'

'Yes.'

'Even though I told you that I feel good and that the shiny guys have gone?'

'I'm afraid I don't fully believe you. You *are* taking your medication?'

'Yes,' I lie.

'I've asked the nurses to keep an eye on you.'

'There's no need.'

Dr Parkinson looks at his watch.

'Is it the end of the session?' I ask.

'It is.'

'Aren't you going to tell me that we're all in it together?'

'A clever attitude like that won't help you get better.'

'You'd prefer it if I were stupid?'

'I'd prefer it if you didn't mock.'

'Okay.'

'And please don't steal any defibrillators. We may need them to start a patient's heart.'

I leave. After all, I have an escape plan to make ready.

I sneak to the gym without being observed, unless there are Nestorians lurking that I don't see. I realise where I will find my rope. The hook in the ceiling is not such a great mystery. There would have been a rope hanging from it, like they have in lots of gyms. Since this gym is in a psychiatric ward, someone was probably worried that the rope might be a suicide risk, so they took it down. But it will have been stashed somewhere convenient, because people never try any harder than they need to.

There is a bank of grey lockers against the wall opposite the basketball hoop. I pick three locks before I find the rope, neatly coiled. I hide the rope under the vaulting horse, where I have been amassing supplies. There are twenty chocolate bars, nine packets of crisps and other things that I've stolen from the vending machine using my magic coin. There are fresh clothes from the laundry. More importantly, I've worked out how Mango, Anthea and I will leave Ward 44.

Barbara with the bazoobies walks briskly by. I tail her, unnoticed. As I suspected, she heads downstairs to smoke, the door propped open. Everything is falling into place.

I return to my bedroom.

I wish I could find *The Castle*. I need to use the joker bookmark. He now has a greater purpose than holding my page for me. I'm convinced that Len stole the book from the cabinet. My deck of playing cards is still there, however. I love my deck, but I will have to sacrifice one card for the escape plan to work.

With the texta I stole from Dr Parkinson's pen caddy, I draw on the back of the ace of spades until the intricate red pattern is completely covered in black. I carefully tear it in half, then into quarters, covering the white tear marks with more black texta. This means I can no longer do parlour tricks with my cards. But I must perform bigger, more elaborate tricks.

Mango has fully recovered from the sedative. He sits, flanked by Anthea and me, in the courtyard. It will soon be time for gym, but I feel confident that my preparations will go unnoticed. The sun is warm and golden. Mango yawns and takes off his pyjama top. He peers down at the flab around his belly, which looks more obvious when he sits.

'I should jog,' he says. 'I'm getting fat.'

The hospital grounds are mostly off-limits to us. You can't jog unless you go round and round the courtyard, which would drive even a sane person mental.

'You're not fat,' says Anthea. 'I'm fat.'

I laugh, and Anthea looks like I've hurt her feelings.

'You're thin and you're beautiful,' Mango says under his breath.

'Thanks, but I'm fat,' Anthea insists.

'Even if you *were* fat you would still be beautiful,' I say.

Mango and I can't convince Anthea, but it feels good to try. This is a rare moment of bliss. I would like to stay in this sunny courtyard with Mango and Anthea forever. But I can't abandon the mission. It will be difficult to explain things to Anthea. At the moment she knows nothing about the intruders from the alternate world. While I'm figuring out the best way to explain things to her, Mango looks longingly at the skinny girl with whom he has fallen in love. Her eyes are closed as she's turned her face up to enjoy the sun. Even if her eyes were open I doubt she could see how much Mango loves her.

I'm startled when Anthea speaks.

'I asked Dr Quayle why you're both in a psychiatric ward.'

Anxious as I am to tell Anthea about the momentous thing we must do, I bide my time.

'What did she say?'

'She said I should ask you.'

'That's reasonable,' says Mango.

Anthea realises she will have to tell her own story before we tell ours.

'Drugs,' says Anthea. 'I'm here because of drugs.'

I can't pretend I'm not disappointed. Most of us in Ward 44 don't like the druggies. But if it bothers Mango, he doesn't show it. He says that in the youth training centre it was easy to get drugs. He smoked dope for a while, but he stopped because it made him stupid, like a cat.

'Cats aren't stupid,' Anthea says. 'Cats are highly intelligent.'

Mango and I agree with Anthea because we know it's what she wants. *Of course* cats are intelligent. They're probably even smarter than dolphins. They're certainly smarter than Val, but so are most items of furniture.

'There's another thing,' Anthea says. 'Only you can't tell anyone else.'

Mango is prepared to do a spit and handshake. Anthea says that his verbal assurance is enough.

'Sometimes I see things. Shadows that aren't there.'

'You see them now?' Mango asks.

'No,' says Anthea. 'That's all I'm telling you for the moment. What about you, Colin? Why are you here?'

'I was dropped as a baby,' I say. 'From a helicopter.'

'Seriously.'

I hesitate. 'Well, I kind of tried to kill myself.'

Anthea doesn't seem surprised. Maybe a lot of her friends try to kill themselves.

'How did you do it?'

'You don't need to know that,' says Mango.

I'm surprised that he can speak so directly to the girl he loves.

'I took some pills,' I say, shrugging. 'It was no big deal.'

'What sort of pills?'

'I don't remember.'

Mango is next.

'I started a riot at a youth training centre,' he says.

'It wasn't his fault,' I add.

Mango quietly continues the story. 'I grabbed one of the supervisors from behind. It wasn't deliberate. It just happens sometimes. And guys started kicking him. They thought it was what I wanted. They didn't stop.'

'What's a youth training centre?' asks Anthea.

'It doesn't matter,' says Mango.

'Is it like a prison?'

'That's all I'm telling you for the moment.'

Another minute passes in silence. Perhaps Anthea hopes to hear more from Mango. But he's afraid that anything else he says might make it difficult for Anthea to fall in love with him. Finally he speaks.

'Colin has a plan,' he says. 'You should listen to him. He has good plans.'

I tell Anthea all about Nestor and the shiny guys. I'm persuasive. I realise it's an incredible story, that very few people would believe, but I'm positive that Anthea does.

CHAPTER 29

Q. Anthea, why have you come to see me? I'm sorry, I don't have much time.

A. It's about Colin.

Q. Yes?

A. I'm worried about him.

Q. Why?

A. He sees things. Not shadows. Really strange things.

Q. What does he see?

A. He has this idea that there are giant cockroaches.

Q. Do you think he was being serious?

A. Yes.

Q. Sometimes it's hard to tell with Colin.

A. I wouldn't be telling you this if I didn't think it was serious.

Q. Of course.

A. He believes the cockroaches abduct people from earth and take them to another planet called next door or something like that. He says they abducted his sister.

Did he really lose his sister?

Q. He did.

A. What happened?

Q. It was on the news. She went missing three years ago. The police have only just made an arrest. They think they may have found the bodies.

A. Bodies?

Q. Five children went missing. Some of the bodies were . . . it was horrible.

A. I think I heard something about this.

Q. It was on the news recently.

A. Poor Colin.

Q. Yes.

A. He really believes in the giant cockroaches, Dr Quayle. He thinks I can see them too, just not so clearly. He says he's wearing special contact lenses that were given to him by *good* cockroaches from another planet, so that he can locate the *bad* cockroaches on earth and wipe them out.

Q. Dr Parkinson is his psychiatrist. I will mention this to him.

A. Don't say I told you.

Q. I promise I won't.

A. If he finds out I told you –

Q. What would happen?

A. Colin would hate me. I don't want him to think I betrayed him. But the thing is, Mango believes him. About the cockroaches, I mean.

Q. Mango is easily influenced. It's not good that Colin is telling him these things. Thank you for coming to me, Anthea. Is there anything else?

A. No.

Q. Are you sure?

A. Yes.

Q. Colin hasn't asked you to do something you don't want to do?

A. No.

Q. We care for him, Anthea. You shouldn't feel that you must protect Colin, even if you –

A. There's nothing else.

CHAPTER 30

Anthea is in her netball trance, shooting basket after basket. I like this expression: *shooting a basket.* I picture a rifle range and see myself killing Len's basket. I might as well kill *him*, he loves it so much. Mango and I sit together on a gym mat, watching Anthea. I'm working out the last few details of the escape plan. Mango gazes at his dream girl. He wears a look of desperate hope. Anthea barely acknowledges either of us.

Barbara with the bazoobies enters.

'Hello, Colin, darlin',' she says. 'Do you think you could come with me for a moment?'

Poor Mango is so besotted with Anthea that Barbara's fantastic bazoobies don't even register. As I leave the gym, I call out to Anthea.

'You should teach Mango how to shoot baskets.'

'Where are you taking me?' I ask Barbara.

'Don't you know? You're goin' to be taken out on

day leave, just like our dear friend Jill with her sister. Your father is waitin' for you.'

My heart misses three beats. 'I'm not ready. I don't like it that I wasn't told.'

'Are you sure you weren't told?'

'I'm in my pyjamas.'

'I noticed that.'

'I can't go out in my pyjamas.'

'Don't you worry. I'm sure that nice day clothes will be provided. I do envy you, Colin.'

'Why would you envy me?'

'You're so young. When I was your age I was one mean basketball player. Seein' Anthea shootin' those baskets brought it all back. Now I'm fifty and my left rotator cuff is like somethin' you'd get out of a Christmas bonbon. I'd give anythin' to be able to play basketball again. I'd have grabbed that ball and slam-dunked it right in front of you and made your eyes pop out. Come on, keep up, honey. I don't know what bad stuff is goin' on in your head, Colin, but I sure hope you're gettin' better. It's not right, a young man like you bein' so troubled. I have two beautiful boys of my own. They're not troubled at all, and you should have seen what *they* had to live through. I can't believe I'm tellin' you all this. You must have one of those faces. Now, where has your father got to?'

We stop at the nurses' station.

'He may have gone to the bathroom,' says Barbara. 'Maybe we should wait here. What is it you like doin' most? Because whatever it is, I expect your dad's planned the whole day around it. He does seem such a pleasant sort of person. Handsome, like you.'

'You don't understand, Barbara. My father doesn't like me.'

'What?'

'He hates me.'

'Oh, baloney. I've seen a hatin' father before, and your daddy isn't one. Why would he want to take you out for the day if he hates you?'

'Nurse Steele,' Shamita calls from the nurse's station. 'Could you please come here?'

Barbara pats me on the arm. 'You just wait a moment, darlin'.'

I smell the cigarettes on Barbara's breath. She smokes one an hour. That means she finished her last cigarette about ten minutes ago. It's important to keep track of things like this. Every bit of information helps.

Barbara and Shamita talk in lowered voices. When the buxom American nurse returns, she looks deflated. Even her proud bazoobies seem to have wilted a little.

'Well, Colin, it seems I've made the most embarrassin' mistake and I'm terribly sorry about it.'

'Dad doesn't want to take me out, does he?'

'Of course he does. I bet he'd like to take you out forever. But right now he's talkin' with Dr Parkinson. It's my mistake. When I saw your dear father standin' there and Shamita told me to fetch you I naturally presumed – well, I was wrong and I hope you can accept my apology.'

'That's okay.'

Shamita frowns at Barbara. I wish she wouldn't. Shamita has a beautiful face. Frown lines will ruin it.

'Dr Parkinson and your father would like to see you,' Shamita tells me.

'Can I just go in?'

'Go right in.'

Dr Parkinson and my father are in the middle of an intense conversation. They stop when I enter. Dad gives me a nervous smile. He looks small.

'Hello, Colin.'

'Hi, Dad. What are you doing here?'

'Your mother would have come too, but she isn't well.'

'What is it?'

'Just a cold. I think she was worried about giving it to you. You've already got enough on your plate. You haven't rung.'

'There hasn't been much to tell you.'

'We were worried when we heard what the security guard did.'

Dr Parkinson jumps in. 'Colin, you should have rung your parents. I asked you to.'

'Yes, I remember. You did ask me. Sorry. And sorry, Dad.'

'You see, we were wondering – your mother and I – we were wondering if maybe this isn't the best place for you.'

Dr Parkinson resents my father's criticism. 'I think you'll find this is one of the best psychiatric units there is. Colin is making process. Aren't you, Colin?'

I nod, not entirely sure of the game that Dad and Dr Parkinson are playing.

'Even so I don't think Colin is ready to leave us just yet,' adds Dr Parkinson.

As they talk, I reach into my slipper and pull out a coin. I try to do an underside walk with it, but I fumble and the coin drops to the floor. It's unlike me to be so clumsy.

'We've been looking at other hospitals,' Dad says. 'I hope you don't mind, Colin?'

I pick up the coin and don't answer.

'We found another ward that seems more . . . appropriate,' Dad continues.

His eyes plead with me to say something, but I don't.

I know Dr Parkinson well enough to see that he is angry. 'In what way *appropriate*?' he says.

'Well, the staff were very helpful,' says Dad, turning to him. 'More traditional. And the patients were wearing their regular clothes.'

'The staff *here* are very helpful,' says Dr Parkinson. 'Isn't that right, Colin? Wouldn't you say the staff are helpful?'

'Very helpful.'

'What is the point of the grey pyjamas?' Dad asks.

Parkinson has often been asked this question, and recites a well-rehearsed reply. 'One of the problems with psychiatric wards is that a pecking order may establish itself. You know as well as I do how quick we are to judge a person by what he wears. You noticed my tie as soon as you walked in. Perhaps you don't even realise it, but it made an impression on you, either good or bad. In a ward where all patients dress alike, there is a sense of unity. All are equal. It's an atmosphere I like to encourage. And patients learn responsibility. They alone must look after what they wear.'

'It doesn't look like a normal hospital,' says Dad.

'It isn't, Mr Lapsley. That's the point. It's the result of many years of study and refinement.'

'It looks like a prison.'

Dr Parkinson has to bite his tongue and pull himself together. He takes a deep breath and says, 'Colin, would you say Ward 44 is a prison?'

I try to do the underside walk with the coin, but drop it again.

'Colin? What do you think.'

Dr Parkinson stops me when I stoop to pick up the coin.

'You don't need to worry about the coin,' he says. 'Please reassure your father that you are not in a prison.'

'I'm not in a prison,' I say.

'And your hallucinations are receding,' says Dr Parkinson. 'You told me yourself only this morning.'

I nod. 'I did tell you that.'

Dad looks at me, then at Dr Parkinson. 'We spoke with other doctors who expressed reservations –'

'I'm more than familiar with professional jealousy,' Dr Parkinson says. 'If you recall, I did take you and your wife on a tour of the ward. I described our methods. I understood you had confidence in me. I even adopted Colin as my own patient, and my other commitments mean I'm restricted in the number of patients I can see. I assure you that Colin's progress –'

The phone on the desk rings. Dr Parkinson picks up the receiver. I hear Dr Quayle's nasal voice.

'I'm sorry, I'll have to ring you back,' says Dr Parkinson. He cradles the receiver.

I pick up the coin.

'You guaranteed that Colin would be safe,' says Dad.

'All of our patients have thorough risk assessments,' says Dr Parkinson.

'Yet Colin was hurt. You were hurt, weren't you, son?'

I turn over the coin in my hand.

In exasperation, Dad takes a letter from his pocket. I recognise Dr Parkinson's signature. Dad shakes his head as though he is still astounded by the contents of the letter.

'A security guard in this ward *electrocuted* my son.'

'I spoke to your wife, Mr Lapsley. She accepted it was an accident. Colin wasn't hurt and the hospital shouldn't be held accountable.'

'Your guard seriously thought he was being attacked by this thin boy?' says Dad, waving his hand at me.

'I believe that Mr Tyler did not act irresponsibly,' says Dr Parkinson. 'I don't wish to discuss this in front of Colin. It was a most unfortunate incident, and there is no point in dwelling on it.'

I open my palm and the coin shines. In that moment I know exactly what to say. I remember standing at the top of the grimy concrete stairs leading to the laundry, wondering if I should hurl myself down them. I chickened out. But now I have the chance to do the right thing by my parents. At last I can be useful.

'Dad, it was agony,' I say.

Dr Parkinson and my father are silent.

I raise my voice. 'It hurt so much I thought I would die. I can show you the mark.'

I pull down my pyjama pants a little, revealing the red crescent made by the Hotshot. Dad reaches out.

'Please don't touch it,' I say. 'It's still very painful.'

Dr Parkinson cuts in. 'Colin what are you saying? We've been through this.'

Dad can't find the words to express what he's thinking. 'Why is there no dressing on this wound?'

'It doesn't *need* dressing,' says Dr Parkinson, so loudly that people outside his office must surely hear. 'It's nothing.'

'Someone uses a cattle prod on my son and you call it nothing?'

'Mr Lapsley, you're being over-dramatic.'

'I've been having nightmares about it,' I say. 'The pain won't go away. You could sue the hospital, Dad.'

Dr Parkinson sighs. 'Colin, I thought better of you.'

'Dad, you could make a lot of money out of this.'

'We don't need money, Colin.'

'Yes, you do. People make thousands from malpractice suits. Hundreds of thousands. I've got the mark. I'll tell everyone how it felt, how I was nearly killed. You and Mum could go on an amazing holiday. You could go to Agra and see the Taj Mahal.'

Dad is not as excited as I hoped he would be. His tone has changed. 'No, Colin. I don't think it would be a good idea to sue the hospital.'

Dr Parkinson and my father look at each other as though a secret understanding has been reached.

'But I was injured –' I protest.

Dad clasps and unclasps his hands. 'The thing is, Colin, it probably isn't a good idea to go telling stories like that.'

'It's the truth. I'll be telling the truth, and you'll be rich.'

'I don't want you to do that. I hate the idea of you being hurt. Of course I do. But I don't want you telling stories that only *might* be the truth. Not after everything that's happened. Not after Briony.' Dad is lost in the nightmare I created for him and Mum by not telling them what I saw at Pichi Richi Pass that day. I know what will follow. He won't be able to stop himself talking, no matter what I say or do. 'It seems so strange that you didn't tell us you saw the man who killed Briony. When the police caught the murderer –'

'Please, Dad.'

'– when they caught the murderer, he told them everything. They couldn't shut him up.'

'Please, Mr Lapsley,' Dr Parkinson interrupts, 'this is not helping.'

'Five kids in all. He has a photographic memory. He described speaking to you at Pichi Richi Pass, before taking Briony away. You *saw* him, Colin. You even *spoke* with him. If you'd told us that when it happened, the police might have saved the other kids. They might have saved Briony.'

'Please, Mr Lapsley.'

'Dad, I swear I didn't remember anything. Not until the police showed me the photographs of the murderer.'

'And now you remember it all? Three years later. How is that possible?'

Dr Parkinson intervenes. 'Colin buried the memory. It's not uncommon. It happens when people suffer a major traumatic experience –'

'But how can it all come back?' Dad says. 'Just like that?'

'The photographs Colin saw acted as a trigger. They shouldn't have been shown to Colin. The police went about it the wrong way.'

My eyes start to water because of the alien contact lenses.

'He told us he was a park ranger,' I say. 'I remember it now. But I couldn't back then. Why didn't I do anything then?'

'I really don't know, Colin.' Dad shakes his head and stares at the floor. 'I don't understand.'

Dr Parkinson speaks softly to him. 'Colin is making progress. He'll be home before long.'

'Yes,' says Dad, without looking up. 'But my little girl won't.'

There's a horrible silence and then Dr Parkinson says, 'We're looking after him, Mr Lapsley. You can be a family again.'

'Yes.'

'And you're feeling well, aren't you, Colin?'

I don't answer. My father wouldn't hear anyway. He averts his eyes from me.

'Colin wasn't hurt by the security guard,' Dr Parkinson says. 'The charge would have been like a mosquito bite. Nothing at all. There's more voltage in the ECT he receives.'

Another awful silence crashes down. I can't believe what I've just heard.

'Dad?'

Nothing.

'Dad?'

Dr Parkinson stands and puts a hand on Dad's shoulder, seeking to comfort him, even though I'm the one who's been kicked in the guts. They have been giving me ECT. How can that be when Mum and Dad haven't given them permission?

I can't remain in the office. As I run out, I hear Dr Parkinson calling for Tim to fetch me.

I run to my room and feel the door of the cabinet beside my bed. It isn't hot. This is not the portal to the infirmary. Not at the moment. It moves around, after all. I try other doors, but they too are cold to the touch. Eventually I find the portal. The door is hot and I strike it with metal, just as Dr Maximew advised.

It opens.

'Colin?'

It's Mango's voice. The water is so hot that vapour fills the shower stall.

'I need the infirmary,' I say.

'What are you doing with a dumbbell?'

'I need the infirmary.'

'Put it down, man. Don't drop it.'

I do as Mango says.

'If you want a shower, use the other one.'

'I need the infirmary. I need to be here. Dr Vendra will be coming.'

I step into the stall.

'Colin, what are you doing?'

'I'll leave my pyjamas on,' I say.

'Don't be crazy.'

'Please, Mango. I need to be here so Dr Vendra can fetch me. It won't take long. He'll be here soon.'

'Okay, Colin. Everything is fine. You don't have anything to worry about.'

CHAPTER 31

I'm finding it harder to climb the stairwell. The steps seem more decayed since my last visit.

'I'm sorry it took me so long to fetch you,' says Dr Vendra.

'Why can't I remember you bringing me here?' I ask.

'Short-term memory loss. It's nothing to be concerned about.'

I stumble and Dr Vendra steadies me.

'You seem to be having difficulty today,' he says.

'I'm just tired, that's all.'

Dr Vendra sighs. 'It has been a busy time here on Nestor. The abducted humans have been relocated. It's a long and arduous process.'

'Where are they?' I ask.

'Colin, how delightful to see you again.'

I look up to see Dr Maximew descending the stairs. This is against the rules. We are on the up stairwell, not the down one. I'm surprised that a cockroach who so admires order should break this elementary law.

'I presume Dr Vendra has told you the good news?' Dr Maximew continues as he approaches.

'I told him,' Dr Vendra says.

'Where are the humans?' I say.

'You will see.'

We stand on the landing of the eighth floor.

'Are they all right?' I ask.

'Yes, yes.'

I take a deep breath and it makes my lungs hurt. 'Can I take one back with me?'

Dr Maximew examines the back of one of his claws, then looks at me. 'You know it's impossible for large things to go from our world to yours.'

'*I* can do it.'

'That's because you *want* to.'

'Briony will want to as well.'

Dr Maximew nods sagely. 'I understand. You are doing such wonderful work, Colin. How can we refuse your request?'

Dr Maximew pushes hard on the big door bearing the number eight.

'Are you sure you're doing the right thing?' Dr Vendra fusses. 'Shouldn't we go to the ninth floor?'

'We must give Colin what he wants, Dr Vendra.'

I help Dr Maximew to open the door.

The eighth floor looks nothing like the one above. There are no narrow corridors with identical doors. It's more like a cavernous warehouse. In the darkness I can make out square shapes on the floor, arranged in a grid.

'Don't be afraid, Colin,' says Dr Maximew.

'I'm not afraid of anything in this world.'

Dr Maximew steps with me over the threshold. Dr Vendra seems nervous as he follows.

'No good can come of this,' he dithers.

Dr Maximew prowls between what I now recognise as packing crates. There must be a thousand of them.

Dr Maximew pauses. 'You needn't be concerned, Colin. The humans are alive. Would you like to see?'

I nod.

Dr Maximew lifts the lid from one of the crates. It's hinged and opens like a door. There is a person in the crate: a girl. But it isn't Briony. Her eyes are closed.

'She is unharmed. She merely sleeps,' says Dr Maximew. 'We rescued her from the recalcitrants.'

'Can you wake her?'

'We could. Is this the person you want to take with you?'

I shake my head. 'Could you open another crate?'

'For you we would do anything.'

Dr Maximew walks ahead of me. His back reflects a light, but I don't know where it's coming from.

'We have worked so terribly hard to bring them all to safety,' says Dr Maximew.

'We have not slept,' adds Dr Vendra, walking behind. His nerves have settled. He sees that I'm calm as I pad slowly through the endless rows of packing crates.

'There are so many,' says Dr Maximew. 'It will be hard to accommodate more. It is vital, Colin, that you stop the abductions. The recalcitrants must be vanquished at all cost. Would you like me to open this crate?'

Dr Maximew points with a delicate claw.

'Yes.'

This crate is not easily opened. Dr Vendra joins Dr Maximew in his efforts to lift the lid. I assist. Together we manage. The person in the crate is at last revealed. This time it's a boy with long curly hair. I recognise him. It's Rodney Meaklin, the kid who disappeared in Anderston.

'Would you like us to wake him?'

'Could we please keep looking?' I say.

We close the lid. Dr Maximew wanders ahead, pointing to various crates. How can I possibly know which one contains Briony? Dr Maximew stops. He holds out two of his arms and points his claws to crates on either side, as if it's a game.

'Left or right?' he asks.

'Left,' I say.

Anticipating that the crate will be hard to open, the three of us lift the lid. We are caught by surprise when it snaps open on its hinge. I look into the crate. A child is lying there. But this child is not complete. The eyes are gone.

'We take your senses: your eyes, ears, nose, mouth and hands,' the cockroach had said.

I cannot speak.

Dr Maximew gently closes the crate.

'I'm so sorry, Colin,' he says. 'It seems we have been betrayed.'

At last I find my voice.

CHAPTER 32

Tim is leaning over me. Mango is there as well. I'm on the gym floor. My pyjamas are wet and there's a blanket over me.

'Colin,' says Mango. 'You blacked out.'

'It's no big deal,' I say.

'Do you feel all right?' Tim asks.

'Where's Dad?'

'He had to go.'

'Can I have some dry pyjamas?'

'I'll get you some,' says Mango. He leaves on his errand.

'Do you want anything else?' asks Tim.

'Just some water please.'

Tim brings a glass of water. I sit up and drink.

The big clock on the wall is stuck at a quarter past eleven. It's been that way since I was admitted. So many things in the ward don't work. I ask Tim the real time and he tells me the clock is actually right. Even a stopped clock is right twice a day.

Does Tim know why I'm on the floor in wet pyjamas? He says he found me like that. I see the big wet footprints leading from the showers to where I'm lying. Mango must have carried me here. I guess when I emerged from the infirmary it was via one of the stall doors. It probably wasn't long ago in earth time, though it seemed I was in Nestor for hours, staggering up those crumbling stairs, finding the crates, opening them. Finding the incomplete child . . .

'Dr Parkinson wants to see you after lunch,' says Tim.

'Okay. But I feel bleary.'

Tim smiles. 'Don't worry.'

I like Tim's smile. 'You are a good nurse,' I say.

Tim sits on the floor beside me.

'It's kind of you to say that, Colin, but I feel I've let you down.'

'That's okay. You apologised when you snapped at me. You were upset that Keith was sacked.'

'The stress has been getting to me. I hope I don't let you down again.'

I take another long drink of water.

'Tim, have I been receiving ECT?' I ask.

Tim is surprised. 'You know you have.'

I swallow. 'I don't remember.'

'Are you absolutely sure?'

'Tell me what happens when I have ECT.'

'Maybe you should talk with Dr Parkinson.'

'I'd rather you explained it. Would that be all right?'

Tim looks at the stopped clock on the wall, as if seeking its permission to speak. 'Colin, are you *positive* you don't remember?'

'Please tell me.'

'Okay. It's the same every time. I take you next door to the waiting room. When everything is ready, another nurse fetches you and takes you into the treatment room.'

'What happens in the treatment room?'

'You lie down on a trolley near the ECT unit, and then the anaesthetist gives you an injection. I shouldn't have to tell you this. It's all been explained.'

I shake my head. 'People have been keeping secrets from me.'

'They haven't, Colin. I'm telling you things I've already told you.'

'Then why don't I remember?'

'Perhaps you should speak with Dr Parkinson.'

'I'd rather talk to you than him.'

'He's the one you should talk to.'

'I'd still rather hear it from you. What happens when I'm injected and I'm lying on the trolley? Do they put a helmet on me or something?'

'They're not mad scientists, Colin. There are just two leads and they put them here and here.' Tim points one finger at the top of his head and the other at his left temple. 'Or sometimes here and here.' He taps both his temples.

'Do they put sticky stuff on me?'

Tim looks relieved and nods. 'Gel. You see, you do remember.'

'How long does it take? How strong is the charge?'

'Ask Dr Parkinson. I don't see you again until you're in the recovery room and you've been given the all clear.'

'Am I like a zombie?'

'Of course you aren't. You're fine. ECT doesn't turn you into a zombie. I walk you back from the recovery room, if I'm rostered on. Sometimes Shamita does it. But I do it if I can. I like talking with you.'

'We talk as we walk?'

'It's not like it's a magic trick, Colin.'

'What do we talk about?'

'What we always talk about. Books mainly.' Tim reaches out and strokes my forehead. 'Colin, you don't know what you were like when they admitted you. I felt so sorry for you. Yours was the deepest depression I've seen, and I've been working here for ten years. ECT *helps*. It's helping *you*.'

'How can you say that when there are so many things I don't remember?'

'Short-term memory loss. That will pass.'

'How can you be sure?'

'I've seen it happen before.'

'But how do you know *exactly* what's happened to my brain? What about when I'm thirty? Or forty? You don't know how I'm going to end up.'

'There are years of research –'

'And you *still* don't know how it works. Does Mango know I've been having ECT?'

'Not unless you told him. You're very close, aren't you?'

'I didn't tell him.'

'Maybe you did and you forgot?'

'No. If Mango knew that you were giving me ECT, he would have stopped you.'

Tim runs his hand through his blond hair. His hairline is receding, but I haven't noticed till now. He's not as young as I thought.

'This can be a depressing place,' says Tim.

'Yes.'

'I can't keep doing the same job. It's embarrassing. My boyfriend is embarrassed. He makes four times the money that I do.'

'Does he work in a psychiatric hospital too?'

Tim is quietly sad. 'Pretty much. He's in advertising. He just got promoted again.'

'Well, maybe they'll give you a promotion here? Can you get a promotion?'

'Yes,' says Tim. 'Yes, I believe I can.'

Mango bounds in, carrying a pair of pyjamas. Tim stands and tries to look professional. He reminds me to see Dr Parkinson after lunch. Then he leaves the gym. When Mango is sure that Tim is out of earshot, he speaks to me.

'Are you okay? When you woke up, you really yelled. I never heard anyone make a noise like that before. You scared the crap out of me.'

'I found out something bad. It's hard to explain.'

'Is it to do with the shiny guys?'

I can't tell Mango what Tim told me about the ECT. I'm not even sure I believe him.

'Yes, it's to do with the shiny guys.'

'Anthea sees black shadows and you see shiny guys.'

'We see the same thing. Anthea doesn't realise because she can't see them properly and I can.' It's good to have a purpose again. I feel my strength returning as I recall the mission. 'They're evil. They have to be stopped.'

I shudder at the memory of the eighth floor. Then I change the subject to something that I know Mango will want to talk about.

'Did Anthea teach you to shoot baskets?'

'She did for a little while,' says Mango. 'But then she left. The thing is, Colin, she prefers you.'

'What? No.'

'She prefers you to me.' Mango is bereft.

'That's not possible,' I say.

'You see what a lucky guy you are? You have nothing to worry about. Are you going to put on these dry pyjamas?' He hands them to me. 'I went all the way to the laundry to get them.'

I immediately drop the pyjamas. 'Mango, did they come out of the dirty laundry skip?'

Mango looks at the stopped clock on the wall. It's what you look at when you don't want to answer a question.

'Yes,' he says.

'I can't wear these. Anyone could have worn them. They might be Len's.'

'Sorry, I didn't have a choice.'

'Why didn't you get the spare pair from my room? In the cabinet beside the bed?'

'Because Len was there.'

'Weren't some of the other rooms empty?'

'I didn't want to ferret around in case I was caught.'

'Why were you afraid of being caught?'

His voice rises. 'I don't know.'

'We'll be out of here soon. You *can't* be afraid.'

'I –'

'If you went to the laundry, why didn't you take clean pyjamas out of the drier and not the skip?'

'The driers don't open when they're working.' Mango grabs a thick tuft of his hair. 'The thing is, Colin . . . I've been concentrating on other stuff. And . . . and you shouldn't be asking me all these questions. I tried to do a good thing for you and you're asking me all these questions like I'm stupid or something. Put the pyjamas on. It doesn't matter who wore them last.'

Anthea has broken Mango's heart and now I'm intimidating him. I hate myself.

'Let me show you something,' I say.

I stand too quickly and I wobble, but manage to stay upright. I leave the dirty pyjamas on the floor and walk over to the vaulting horse. I want to lift it dramatically to reveal what's stashed underneath, but I'm too weak for stagecraft.

'Could you help me with this?'

Mango wanders over. He tells me to stand aside and lifts the horse at one end, revealing the booty underneath. There are chips, chocolate bars, chewing gum and a big biscuit made from muesli. Mango's disgusting pair of dirty pyjamas and the fresh clothes that I stole from the tumble driers are also there.

Mango is thrilled. 'Man, there must be a hundred dollars worth of stuff here.'

'They're supplies. For when we escape,' I say.

I take out the chocolate bar and Mango's disgusting pair of pyjamas.

'You can lower it now,' I say.

Mango lowers the horse and I hand him a chocolate bar.

'Don't tell anyone.'

Mango unwraps the chocolate bar. 'What are you going to do with the pyjamas?'

'Change into them,' I say.

Mango looks horrified. 'But they're the most disgusting pyjamas in the universe. They're mine.'

I nod. 'I don't mind.'

CHAPTER 33

There's a glass of water, two yellow tablets, two blue tablets and five capsules on Dr Parkinson's desk.

'I'm sorry about what happened with your father,' says Dr Parkinson.

'Where is he?' I ask.

'I explained a few things to him and set his mind at ease. He's gone home.'

'What did you explain exactly?'

'Complicated things.'

'What exactly?'

'Disassociation. Repressed memory. Colin, I'd like you to do the trick where you make my pencil turn into rubber. You didn't do a very good job before.'

'Sure.'

I take the pencil from the caddy and drop it before I even get a chance to shake it.

'Show me another trick. The one where you hold out your palms, I put the coin in your right palm, you flip your hands onto the desk and the coin ends up under your left.'

'If you like.'

I hold out my palms and I'm surprised to see how much they shake. Dr Parkinson does not give me a coin.

'You can put your hands down now.'

I place them on the desk, and yet they still tremble.

'When did you stop taking your medication?'

I'm disappointed in myself. I obviously haven't been clever enough with my palming. I'm not as good a magician as I thought I was.

'Who told you I stopped taking it?'

'No one did, Colin. It's obvious.' Dr Parkinson pushes the glass of water towards me. 'How long has it been since you took your medication?'

'A few days.'

'I need to know exactly.'

'I'm not sure.'

Dr Parkinson shakes his head slowly, as if I am an errant little kid and there is no hope for me. 'Why did you stop?'

'Someone told me to.'

'Who told you?'

'It's kind of difficult to explain.'

'Try.'

'Dr Parkinson, I need to talk with you about the ECT.'

'Right now I need to know who told you not to take the tablets. Was it another patient?'

'It wasn't a patient.'

'It can't have been your parents. You saw how concerned your father is.'

I shake my head. 'He still blames me.'

'He doesn't.'

'They both do.'

'They don't. You must understand that. There are
just one or two things they don't fully comprehend, but
they will. I'm going to watch you take the tablets now.
No conjuring tricks, please. Don't hide them in your
hand. You're going through withdrawal. It's dangerous.
I'd say it's been more than a few days since you stopped
taking the tablets. Take them now. You'll feel drowsy.
Tim will take you straight to bed. I promise that when
you wake up you'll be feeling a lot better.'

'Before I take the tablets –'

'Yes?'

'My parents signed the form, didn't they?'

'Which form?'

'For the ECT.'

'Ah. Yes.'

'They told me they didn't.'

'Please take the tablets, Colin.'

I raise the glass. There's a reflection in the water. A
Nestorian face leers. It's as if the monster is looking over
my shoulder. I drop the glass to the floor and spin around
but there is nothing. When I turn back, Dr Parkinson
looks unflustered.

'What made you do that?'

I pick up the glass and place it, empty, on the desk.
'Sorry.'

'What did you see in the glass?'

'Nothing.'

'Was it the usual hallucination? Something to do with the shiny guys?'

I don't answer.

Dr Parkinson is distressed. 'Oh, Colin. I wish you hadn't stopped taking the medication. Who told you not to? Was it one of the shiny guys?'

I still don't answer.

'I'll get you more water.'

The phone on the desk rings and Dr Parkinson picks up. It is Dr Quayle again.

'I can't talk now,' says Dr Parkinson.

Dr Quayle is insistent.

'Please, we'll talk later.'

Dr Parkinson hangs up.

'Don't worry,' I tell him. 'I can take the tablets without water.'

'Then do it now, please. And when you wake up, I want you to ring your parents.' Dr Parkinson puts his hands together to make a steeple. 'We've all been a bit foolish. You shouldn't have stolen from the ward. I shouldn't have overreacted and employed Mr Tyler, though in my defence I didn't realise that Keith had told him horror stories. The last thing I expected was that he'd be carrying that stupid stick. He was an idiot to use it on you, but I must take ultimate responsibility. I'm very sorry about what happened.'

'That's okay.'

'You weren't hurt.'

'Not much.'

'You weren't hurt. Not at all. I want to show you something.'

Dr Parkinson unbuttons his shirt sleeve. He rolls back the sleeve till it is past his elbow. I see his bicep, which is white and flabby. There is a red crescent shape.

'You got Hotshot,' I say.

'Yes.'

I'm amazed. 'Who did it?'

'I did.'

'Dr Parkinson, are you a self-harmer? That's probably bad for a psychiatrist.'

Dr Parkinson rolls down his sleeve and buttons his cuffs. 'I needed to know how bad the pain was. I wanted to feel what *you* felt.'

'Did it hurt?'

'Not at all.'

'Is it the same Hotshot that Pete used?'

'It's the same type.'

'Do you still have it?'

'No. You'll just have to believe me. If I didn't feel anything, neither did you.'

'Maybe Pete used a higher setting?'

'Colin, if you lie, if you tell people you *were* hurt, you will be opening a can of worms. It won't turn out well.'

I picture myself with a can-opener; freeing hundreds of worms and having them squirm up my arms. It's a sickening thought.

'Have you told anyone else to stop taking their medicine?' Dr Parkinson asks.

'No.'

'You haven't told Malcolm? I know how close you are.'

It's the same expression that Tim used. I must look puzzled.

'Colin, it really doesn't matter,' says Dr Parkinson.

'What doesn't matter?'

'I'm actually happy for you.'

'What are you talking about?'

'You're in a . . . physical relationship with Malcolm, aren't you?'

I'm used to Len saying I'm a poofter, but I didn't think Dr Parkinson would.

'No,' I say. 'We look out for each other. That's all.'

'You were in the shower together, embracing. Tim saw you. I have no problem, Colin. In some ways, Malcolm may be immature, but I'm confident that he's . . . willing.'

'We weren't doing anything.'

'Why were you in the shower together?'

I say nothing. I don't want to tell Dr Parkinson about portals and the alternative world.

'I'll have to speak with Malcolm about it,' says Dr Parkinson, enjoying the idea that Mango and I are on together, 'but I'm sure that you aren't exploiting him.'

'I didn't even take my pyjamas off.'

'Of course you did.'

'Then how come they were wet?'

'Because you left them on the bench inside the stall

when you got undressed. It's a ridiculous arrangement. Everything gets wet. I've often complained about it. You put the wet pyjamas back on after you and Malcolm were done.'

'That's bullshit.'

'I'm concerned that you're so upset about this.'

'I'm not upset. It's just bullshit, that's all.'

'Whose pyjamas are you wearing now?'

'Mine.'

'You're not normally so messy. Are you sure?'

'They're mine.'

Dr Parkinson knows that I'm wearing Mango's pyjamas.

'Colin, if your intimacy with Malcolm is consensual, it need not concern us. And I certainly won't inform his parents. Though if you open that can of worms –'

'Mango doesn't have parents.'

'He does.'

I shake my head. 'You're wrong. They died.'

'They are very much alive.'

'Describe them.'

'Well, they are . . . just ordinary people, I suppose. Perhaps not as broad-minded as some. A bit intolerant. Maybe racist. Definitely homophobic. Please take the medication.'

I put all the pills and capsules under my tongue and gulp. After I leave Dr Parkinson's office, I go to the toilet and spit them out.

Tim is treacherous to make up stories about Mango and me. Why would he do this? Can he really be so desperate for a promotion that he would lie to Dr Parkinson? Is it something they've cooked up together, a way to protect the good name of Ward 44? They're all liars. If Mango's parents are alive, he would have told me.

I continue with the escape plan. Barbara leaves the nurses' station and I follow her, chewing the gum that I stole from the vending machine. Downstairs in the laundry, she takes off one of her shoes. Using her key-card, she opens the exit door then props it open with the shoe. The desperation of smokers amazes me. Barbara is prepared to stand outside wearing one shoe, so she can get her nicotine rush.

The tumble driers rumble on. I creep over to the exit door. On the frame there's a small rectangular hole where the tongue from the lock clicks into place. I take the gum from my mouth and produce a torn black piece of card that used to be my beloved ace of spades. With the gum, I stick the card over the rectangular hole, making sure it lies as flat as possible. It's invisible, the black card that will obstruct the lock. Barbara will come in and let the door swing shut. What she won't realise is that, although it's closed, it's not locked. And since she's about to go off duty, she won't find out that a magician has performed a neat little trick. I hope Barbara doesn't get into trouble. I like her. She isn't like Tim or Len or Dr Parkinson. She doesn't scheme.

There's a bin near the door. I've never noticed it before. It contains empty pillboxes, blister packs and other rubbish. I realise that I didn't need to spoil my deck of cards. I could have used cardboard from one of the boxes to do my trick. I grab one of the boxes, then hear Barbara butting out her cigarette, so I flee.

In the courtyard I tell Mango and Anthea that we're escaping tonight. We'll meet in the gym at nine o'clock, when the night lights come on. We'll change into the clothes I've hidden under the vaulting horse, gather the rope and supplies, and then exit via the ground floor. Anthea looks doubtful. I gaze into her eyes and tell her it's *vital* that she joins us. I can beat the Nestorians and save the earth, but I will need her help. I still have the pillbox I salvaged from the bin downstairs. I turn it over and over in my magic hands.

'Is the box part of the escape plan?' asks Mango.

I see the name of the pharmaceutical company on the box: Maximew and Vendra.

Coincidences happen.

'No,' I say. 'It isn't part of the plan.'

'I'm not coming with you,' says Anthea.

'You have to,' says Mango.

'Why?'

'Because I want you to,' he says.

'That isn't a good enough reason.'

'If you don't,' says Mango softly, 'I'll kill myself. And if you tell anyone about the escape plan and they stop it, I'll also kill myself.'

It scares me to hear him talk like this.

Anthea agrees to join us.

*

I rifle through my bedside cabinet. *The Castle* by Franz Kafka has definitely been stolen. I ask Len once again if he knows anything about it.

'Let me think,' says Len. 'I believe I *did* see it.'

He pauses for effect. I look at his beloved basket.

'I remember now,' says Len. 'I accidentally dropped it in the toilet. Then I accidentally took an enormous crap on it. That's right. It's all coming back to me.'

When Len falls asleep, I creep over to his bed and take his basket.

I hope 99 will forgive me for breaking into her library. I don't try to hide my crime. My fingerprints will be all over the book press, but by the morning I'll be far away.

I turn the handle that opens the press until it won't turn anymore. There isn't quite enough room for Len's basket. I try to bend it out of shape so I can stuff it into the press, but the basket is so well made that it resists me. Despite all it represents, and the pig that made it, the basket is a thing of beauty and craftsmanship. I squeeze it like a Bullworker. At last it gives, and I can wedge it under the platen. I turn the handle. The basket creaks and groans as the machine crushes it. Its skeleton snaps. Pieces of rattan splinter. The handle of the press becomes harder to twist, but I'm determined to destroy the only thing that Len truly loves.

When I can twist the handle no further, I sit panting on the floor behind 99's desk. I consider leaving her a note about what happened to *The Castle*, but decide not to. What good would it do? You can't bring something back when it's gone.

I place the destroyed basket alongside Len's bed. It's a shame I won't be there to see the old bastard's death throes when he wakes up tomorrow.

CHAPTER 34

Leaving Ward 44 is too easy. Changing out of our pyjamas into casual clothes belonging to the ward staff and their families is not very exciting either, although I could add a bit of sexual tension by saying that when we took off our pyjamas we all looked at one another in a hungry, longing way. But I don't remember that happening.

After the most undramatic escape in history, we run across the hospital grounds. I am carrying a pillowslip containing our supplies: the rope and the stuff I stole from the vending machine. We stop at the fence on the perimeter to catch our breath. I suspect that the t-shirt I wear belongs to Tim. There is a girly rainbow on it. Anthea has one with a picture of Madonna. She wears kids' jeans and they fit her well. You can see she's not happy about escaping, but she doesn't want Mango to commit suicide. For this alone I love her. Mango's shirt is a souvenir from Bali. I wonder which of the nurses is rich enough to go to Bali. Tim is always going on about how nurses can't afford luxuries, but Mango and I are wearing jogging shorts that must have cost at least twenty dollars so someone is lying.

Mango is strong. He doesn't need the rope to get over the fence. He climbs effortlessly. His penis falls out of his loose psycho-undies and dangles from his shorts. When he's safely over and has tucked his penis back in, he tells us to throw over the supplies. Anthea takes the bundle from me and shoots it over the fence, into Mango's arms. I tell Mango to grab one end of the rope, and throw the other over the fence so that Anthea and I can scale it.

'Man, you don't need a rope,' says Mango. 'Just climb over. The fence isn't that high.'

'But I went to a lot of effort –'

'You still don't need it.'

'It isn't much of an escape without a rope.'

'Colin, don't be mental.'

Anthea is already halfway over. I'm glad she went before me. I'm worried that my penis will fall out of my shorts too, and I don't want her to see that.

We've achieved the first part of the plan and I'm excited beyond belief. We're no longer on hostile ground.

'You're shaking,' says Mango. 'Are you okay? Do you see anything bad?'

'It's clear,' I say. 'I don't see anything.'

'Did you see my dick fall out?' asks Mango.

'No,' I say.

'No,' says Anthea, even though she did.

Mango gives a sigh of relief. It would be mortifying

for Anthea to see his penis as well as his arse, at least until he wants her to. 'What do we do now?'

'Steal a car,' I say. I want it to sound casual and off-hand, as though it's something I say every day, but my voice comes out loud.

Anthea gives me a strange look. 'Are you okay, Colin?'

'Of course I'm okay.'

We pad through the night, nervous when we see people out walking. Then I remember that we don't look like escapees. We're dressed like civilians, even though we're wearing slippers and Mango is carrying provisions in a pillowslip. He's already eaten two packets of crisps, though I've told him they should be rationed.

In a side street we find an old Honda that I don't even need to break into. It's unlocked. I can't believe our luck. Anthea doesn't seem so surprised. I hotwire it easily and start the engine. I step aside so that Mango can climb into the driver's seat. Anthea sits alongside him, and I get in the back. But Mango stalls the car when he tries to drive off. I have to hotwire it again. When the car starts the second time, I notice shapes in the darkness. I shiver.

The Nestorians gather at the end of the side street. A swarm of them approaches, their red shells gleaming in the night.

'We have to go,' I say.

'You see them?' says Mango.

'We have to go *now*.'

I look out of the rear window. The swarm is huge,

a seething mass. There are more than a hundred. There may even be three hundred. The Nestorians want to abduct the three of us. I can see the cockroach eyes, red and cold and glimmering. Our enemies draw closer and closer. Mango flips the car into gear and we move at last. We turn into a main street and build up speed. The cockroaches are left behind. I cry out in victory and Mango asks me not to do that because he has to concentrate on driving.

'There were hundreds of them right behind us,' I say. 'Anthea, did you see them?'

'No,' says Anthea.

'But you felt them, didn't you?' I say. 'You felt something. You must have known the shadows were there?'

Mango cuts in. 'We have to get more food.'

'We will,' I say. 'We need to go to Anthea's place first.'

'What? Why?' cries Anthea.

'You have to ask your dad where we can find some Hotshots.'

'How come you're talking so quickly?'

'Am I talking quickly?'

'You are.'

'I'll try to slow down.' I take a deep breath. 'Anthea, you have to tell your dad how *serious* things are. He's a police officer, so he'll know where to get Hotshots. We need them to kill the Nestorians.'

'My dad doesn't trust me.'

'*Make* him trust you. Tell Mango how to get to your house.'

I feel itching all over my body.

'There's a 7-11,' says Mango.

'Please can we go to Anthea's house first?' I say. 'You don't know how lucky we were to escape the Nestorians. They were practically jumping on the roof.'

'Okay,' says Mango. 'But calm down, man.'

Mango takes a hand off the steering wheel and reaches across to Anthea. She holds his hand gently, and then lets go. After all, Mango has to concentrate.

Anthea's house is in a nice street. Mango brings the car to a halt under the trees.

Anthea hesitates before climbing out.

'Dad won't be happy about this.'

'Tell him it's urgent,' I say.

'He'll be angry that I'm not in hospital.'

'This is more important. You'll be able to convince him. You're amazing.'

'I'm not.'

'You are,' says Mango.

I can hear Anthea breathing as she contemplates.

'Okay, both of you stay here.'

Mango and I watch as she walks to the house. Why does she have to be so slow? She doesn't even go to the front door. She wanders around the back.

'We should have asked Anthea to get food as well as Hotshots,' says Mango.

In the back seat, I sit with my knees tucked under my chin, and my arms enfolding my legs, so that I am like a ball. I rock gently.

'Man, you're shivering,' says Mango, looking back at me.

'I'm okay.'

'You really think Anthea's dad will be able to help?'

'That's why we're here.'

'I hate being in love with her. She isn't in love with me.'

'She was holding your hand.'

'She prefers you.'

'No, she doesn't. You don't have anything to worry about.'

Mango scratches his head. 'Back at the hospital, I really believed there *was* nothing to worry about, except for dreams. Now we're outside, I don't feel so good.'

'We will find the impossible cupboard,' I say. 'We will find it and destroy it and it won't bother you ever again. I'm sorry if I've been behaving like a jerk tonight. I'm feeling strange because I stopped taking the medication. It's made me extra-alert. Please don't be jealous about Anthea preferring me. It's not true.'

'It is.'

'Even it *is* true, you can't stop liking me, Mango, because if you do, it would kill me.'

'Should I turn off the engine?'

'Keep it running. Otherwise I'll have to hotwire it again and my hands are kind of wobbly. I don't know if I could do it.'

The car idles. We wait. The street is dark and empty. The street lights don't penetrate through the treetops.

'Colin, why did you come into the shower?' Mango says.

'It's what I said before. There are portals to Nestor.

They're like two doors, close together but in different dimensions.'

'How close?'

'Thirty centimetres.'

'You never left the shower. You just held me and closed your eyes. You didn't go anywhere.'

'It might have seemed like that to you.'

'It *was* like that. And you kept saying sorry. That's all you did, before you passed out.'

My teeth chatter. 'Is it freezing cold?'

'No. It's warm.'

'I feel cold.'

I find a jumper on the back seat and pull it on with difficulty; I'm trembling so much. Mango looks over the driver's seat and sees me struggle.

'Man, I'm worried about you. I want to take you back to the hospital.'

'I'm fine. I'm warm now.'

'You don't look so good.'

I wipe my nose on the jumper's sleeve. 'Mango, you know I would do anything for you.'

'Sure. We look out for each other. We always will.'

'I would never let anything bad happen to you.'

'I know that. You're still shivering, man.'

His breath smells of potato crisps.

'If someone evil tried to take you away, I would do whatever I could to stop them,' I say.

'I know. I trust you. You're a good person.'

I shake my head.

'You are the best person I know,' says Mango.

'When Briony was abducted,' I say, 'I saw it happen. And I didn't do anything to stop it. All I did was pass out. I didn't tell anyone about it until it was years too late. I didn't mean to . . . but I just wiped out what happened in the forest. I wiped out the man with the sunglasses and the red leather jacket and the canvas shoes. I didn't remember any of it until the police caught him. And I'm sorry. I'm so sorry.'

I cry into the jumper and smell petrol.

'I want to take you back to the hospital,' says Mango.

'We're not going back.'

'Let me take you.'

'They've been electrocuting me, Mango. They've been giving me ECT. When Tim tells me not to eat, it's because of the injections they give me before the treatment.'

'Why didn't you tell me?'

'I didn't know.'

'How can you not know something as big as that?'

I don't answer. I have a theory, about holes in my memory, but it's too horrible to say out loud.

'I would've stopped them,' says Mango.

He rests his head back. His shaggy hair is long, and some of it falls over the back of the seat.

'I'll make Anthea love you,' I say. 'I can do that.'

Mango seems in a daze. 'Two doors. Close together.'

'But in different dimensions.'

'I think I understand.'

After a while, Anthea returns. She's carrying a cat.

'This is Simon,' she says.

'What did your dad say?' I ask.

'My parents aren't home,' she says.

'How come you were gone so long?'

'I kept knocking but no one answered.'

'Then we have to wait. They'll probably be home soon. We need your dad's help.'

'I think they're away on holiday.'

Anthea steps into the car with Simon.

'How can they be on holiday if your cat is still around?'

'They've gone away, all right?' says Anthea.

There can be no further argument.

'Get in the back seat,' Mango tells Anthea. 'I won't be able to drive with the cat alongside me.'

'Where are we going?' I ask.

'It's not far away,' says Mango. 'It's somewhere to sleep.'

I swap places with Anthea. Simon doesn't like the strange car and he yowls.

'Man, I'm tired,' says Mango.

'We should sleep at Anthea's house,' I say.

'No,' says Anthea.

It begins to rain. Simon doesn't like that either, and makes whining noises. Anthea tries to keep him calm. It takes Mango a moment or two to find the control for the windscreen wipers, and then we drive off.

CHAPTER 35

Dear Simon,

It's hard to write in the dark. Because you're a cat, you can see better than I can the paper I have to use. It's from the hospital and it has creases because I folded it and put it in my slipper. Colin taught me to do that. The pen is also from the hospital, which is why it doesn't work very well.

From where I sit I can see Mum and Dad in the kitchen. They're probably arguing about me, trying to work out whose fault it is that I ended up how I am. They were on their best behaviour when they came to the hospital. It must have been hard for them, keeping a lid on. I know Dad hates me. It looks bad for a policeman when his daughter screws up. I promise to stay away from drugs this time. I really promise. I never liked any of those people anyway.

I didn't want to escape from the hospital, but I am doing it because I was afraid that Mango might kill himself if I didn't. I'm safe, so don't worry. Mango and Colin are waiting in the car for me. The registration number is on the back of this note. Colin isn't well. Mango is a good driver, though, and he won't let anything happen.

Mum and Dad have locked you out. I don't like it when they do that. I'll have to take you with me. But I'll leave the note. I think that's best.

xxA

CHAPTER 36

The mission has failed. We didn't find weapons. I'm racking my brain to work out what to do next. We're travelling in the rain, through the outer suburbs. I was so alert before. Now it hits me how tired I am. I nearly pass out on Mango's shoulder.

'I don't mind,' he says.

'Where are you taking us?'

'A place I remember.'

'We're not going back to the hospital?'

'No. You have nothing to worry about. This is my plan now.'

We turn into a bumpy road without streetlights. It doesn't seem like a proper road at all. Mango turns off the headlights and drives up a hill, in darkness.

Mango parks outside a small building and tells us to get out. He wants Anthea to leave Simon in the car. Just open the window a crack. Anthea doesn't want to abandon Simon, but she realises that Mango is the boss now.

The rain is pelting. We shelter under the eaves of the strange building. It's nothing like Anthea's house. It's a bungalow with two windows, several metres apart. They look as though they've been salvaged from another building, rather than purpose-built for the bungalow. It's hard to tell in the poor light, but it looks like it's made from fibro.

'It belongs to my parents,' says Mango.

'Your parents?' I guess Dr Parkinson wasn't lying about that.

'They live further up the hill. There's an old house there. This is the granny flat. But Granny never lived here.'

'How do we get in?' Anthea asks, huddling against the rain.

'I break a window and I let you in,' says Mango, matter-of-factly.

'That'll make too much noise,' I say. 'Let me pick the lock.'

'My parents won't wake up and you won't be able to pick the lock,' says Mango. 'Give me the jumper.' He puts out his hand.

Anthea helps me to take off the jumper and Mango wraps it around his arm. He punches a pane of glass and breaks it, then reaches in to unlock the window. He slides it open, tosses the jumper to Anthea and climbs through.

I hear them before I see them. They scuttle up the hill. Rain pelts on their shiny red backs. There are hundreds in the swarm, and they are malevolent.

I point. 'Look!'

Anthea stares where I point.

'There's nothing.'

I step into the rain. 'They're coming up the hill.'

'Colin, there's nothing there.'

'You can't see them properly. You don't have the lenses.'

The storm grows more violent. If I think hard enough perhaps I can control lightning. It's the only thing that can stop the Nestorians. The tallest cockroach leads the shimmering army. He smiles. He believes that I pose no threat, for I alone cannot make lightning. But if Anthea could see what I see, perhaps we can do it together? I try to remove the lens from my eye.

'Colin, what are you doing?'

'If you wear this lens –' I pick at it.

'Colin, stop. You'll pull out your eye.'

'It's a contact lens. I can get it out. You'll see the Nestorians.'

Anthea pulls my hands away from my face. She won't let go.

'They are not there,' she yells above the storm. 'I promise you, Colin, there is *nothing there*.'

A tremendous flash of lightning lights up the world. For a moment I see the trees bending in the wind. The shining monsters scurry into the night, vanquished for the moment.

Anthea lets go of my hands and I nearly pass out, but she reaches out again and holds me.

'Don't fall asleep,' she says. 'Not yet.'

'I'm freezing.'

Anthea leads me under the eaves of the bungalow, where it's dry. She helps me to put on the jumper.

'Is that better?'

'I'm still freezing.'

Anthea holds me tight. She rubs my back. I rub hers as best I can.

'We can sleep here,' says Mango.

Mango is standing at the open door.

'Come on,' he says, 'get out of the rain.'

Anthea and I enter the fibro house with one broken windowpane.

The roof is leaking. Mango finds a torch with a dull yellow beam. There are Hessian sacks on the floor, some old blankets. We're in a room full of junk, some of it unrecognisable in the torch's faint glow. There's an old-fashioned sewing machine with a treadle. There are mouldering cardboard boxes full of stuff, piled precariously on top of one another. There is nothing that resembles a bed. We'll have to make do with the sacks, of which there are plenty. The blankets look as though they are out of a removal van. They haven't been used for warmth in a long time.

'Can I please get Simon?' asks Anthea.

Mango doesn't like Simon; he doesn't like cats at all. 'No,' he says.

'Mango,' I say, 'Anthea is worried about Simon. She loves her cat. If you loved Anthea, you'd let her fetch him. You'd give her the torch, so she doesn't trip over and hurt herself on the way.'

'Don't shame me,' says Mango.

'I'm just saying, if you really loved Anthea –'

'Go and get the cat,' Mango tells Anthea. In a gentler voice he adds: 'I'm sorry. Please get him.'

'I was going to anyway,' says Anthea.

'Take the torch,' says Mango.

'I don't need the torch. I can see in the dark.'

'I'll come with you.'

'No, I'm fine. Thanks anyway,' Anthea says, leaving to fetch her pet.

Mango shines the torch around the room.

'Did you live in this place?' I ask.

'No one lived here. I wasn't allowed in. This is my parents' stuff.'

'You told me you didn't have parents.'

'Not for a long time,' says Mango.

We poke around, hoping to find something more comfortable than the sacks to sleep on.

'When was the last time you were here?'

Mango shrugs. 'I can't remember.'

I feel the coin in my slipper.

'I'm sorry about this, Mango. I screwed up.'

He shrugs. 'It's okay.'

'Maybe tomorrow you guys should go back to the hospital. But I can't.'

'Where will you go?'

'I don't know. I can't go home.'

'Yes you can. I want you to.' Mango is imploring.

I shake my head. It's beginning to hurt. 'My parents –'

'Oh, Colin. You're so wrong about your parents. They want you back.'

'They don't. They blame me for what happened to Briony and the other kids.'

'Stop saying that, man. I see it when they visit. They want you back so much. You really don't know how lucky you are to have parents like them.'

The room is not as wide as the outside of the bungalow, and it has only one window. There must be another room beyond an adjoining wall. There's a door in the wall, with a knob and an old Yale lock. The key is there. Mango keeps the torch trained on the lock and stares at it.

'What's the matter?' I ask.

Mango slowly turns the key and opens the door. It doesn't make sense. The doorframe doesn't lead into another room. On the other side of the frame is a second locked door with a knob. A door on either side of a doorframe with a narrow space between them.

A space that shouldn't exist.

Mango grabs me from behind. The torch drops from my hand and we lie together on the floor.

CHAPTER 37

'Me and a mate were watching Dad's pornos,' Mango says. 'He used to keep them on top of the wardrobe, as if I wouldn't find them there. I don't know how old we were, still in primary school. Dad and Mum came home early and found us. My mate freaked and ran. He left some of his clothes behind. I remember that. He had better clothes than me. Everyone did.'

Anthea enters. Simon is happier and no longer whines. Anthea sees the glimmer of torchlight and comes over to us. She lies behind Mango and holds him while he holds me. We're like three spoons.

'Dad didn't turn off the porno. It kept going as he hit me over and over. I was small. My punches and kicks were pathetic. But I knew how I could hurt him. I kicked the television so hard it almost exploded. Everything went quiet. No one could believe what I'd done. The television was such an important thing, but I'd killed it with just one kick. Dad and Mum couldn't speak. They dragged me out of the house and down the hill, to the granny flat where Granny never lived.'

Simon wanders over and sits, purring.

'They put me in there,' says Mango. 'They locked me in the space between the two doors. This was the punishment for little perverts who destroyed things. I like it when you hold me, Anthea.'

Simon purrs more loudly.

'I don't think Dad made it deliberately when he built the granny flat. The space between the doors was an accident. He hadn't meant to create a cupboard. But because he and Mum took me straight here, because they knew exactly where they were going, they must have already thought about how to use it. Maybe they thought they never *would* use it. But I did a terrible crime. Are you okay, Colin? I'll be able to let go of you soon.'

'I'm okay, Mango.'

'I tried turning the knobs on each of the doors, but they were locked. I was trapped. I gave up yelling after a while. Our neighbours are too far away to hear. The only people who could hear would be Mum and Dad. I waited for them to let me out. I figured they might leave me there for an hour or something, to teach me a lesson. They'd come for me soon.'

Suddenly Simon gets up and scampers away.

'It's probably a mouse,' Mango says. 'Are you freaked by mice?'

'No,' says Anthea.

'No,' I say.

Mango breathes slowly. 'But they didn't come. They

left me in the impossible cupboard. I thought I would die in there. I was so hungry and thirsty. Everything hurt. I didn't know when I was sleeping and when I was awake.'

Simon has caught the mouse and is playing with it. The mouse doesn't have long.

'Then one day Mum let me out. The light was blinding. I couldn't believe I was alive. As soon as I was out of there, I grabbed hold of Mum. I couldn't let her go, though I wanted to, more than anything.'

Mango relaxes his hold.

'I think I'm big enough now,' he says. 'I can go up the hill.'

'Stay for a bit longer,' says Anthea. 'We don't have to let go.'

'I like it when you hold me,' Mango says.

'We don't have to let go,' Anthea says.

'Just for a bit longer,' I say.

The torchlight goes out.

When I wake I sit up carefully. Mango and Anthea are facing each other, asleep in each other's arms. They look beautiful together; two lovers entwined. A soft golden light plays across them. I've worked my magic and I'm so happy for them that it takes me a moment to realise.

The portal is here. The golden light is coming from under the door that forms the back of the impossible cupboard. I reach out and feel it with a fingertip. The door is hot. I pick up the dead torch and gently tap on the wood. Almost immediately, the door opens. It's Dr Vendra. He looks as though he's about to speak, but I hold a finger to my lips and indicate Mango and Anthea. Simon lies at their feet, his three tails curled about his body.

Dr Vendra beckons with an elegant claw and I walk through the portal.

'It was a memory you buried,' he whispers. 'What happened to Briony was not your fault. Your parents are beginning to understand.'

I breathe the still, smoky air of Nestor, not sure what to say.

'There will always be evil forces in the world,' says Dr Vendra. 'You, Colin, are not one of them.'

Dr Vendra's cockroach body drops from him like dust and I find myself looking at Briony. She's beaming and complete, a miracle.

My eyes water and I try to wipe them, but the tears won't stop.

'Forgive me,' I say.

'There's nothing to forgive,' she says.

'I'm sorry. I'm so sorry.'

'You don't need to say that anymore.'

'Can I stay with you?'

'No. You have other things to do.'

'Please?'

'Let me read something to you.'

Briony plucks a familiar book from the air. She turns to the final page and speaks the words:

'*She held out a tremulous hand to K. and made him sit down beside her, she spoke with an effort, it was difficult to understand her, but what she said –*'

Briony closes the book.

'What?' I ask.

'That's all there is.'

'What happens next?'

'You already know, Colin. You've been told.'

'What happens?'

Briony smiles. 'Metamorphosis.'

The Life of a Teenage Body-Snatcher
DOUG MCLEOD

*'You must think it strange that I'm digging up
my grandfather.'*
*'Not at all. I'm sure many young men dig up
their grandfathers.'*

Thomas Timewell is sixteen and a gentleman. When he meets a body-snatcher called Plenitude, his whole life changes. He is pursued by cutthroats, a gypsy with a meat cleaver, and even the Grim Reaper. More disturbing still, Thomas has to spend an evening with the worst novelist in the world.

A very black comedy set in England in 1828, The Life of a Teenage Body-snatcher shows what terrible events can occur when you try to do the right thing. 'Never a good idea,' as Thomas's mother would say.

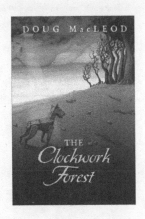

The Clockwork Forest

DOUG MACLEOD

'Life would be a great deal easier if dead things had the decency to remain dead.'

Nothing is how it seems in the forest. Your best friend may turn out to be your worst enemy. A deadly poison might save your life. And two smiling children could become the most horrifying monsters of all.

Funny and sinister, Doug MacLeod is scarily good.